I0688630

Other Works

MASHED: The Culinary Delights of Twisted Erotic Horror (anthology; editor Grivante)

Tales from the Boiler Room (anthology)

FINDERS BLEEDERS

FINDERS BLEEDERS

J. Donnait

EPIC PUBLISHING
Pittsburgh

First Printing: 2020

ISBN 978-1-7320013-9-8

Special discounts are available on quantity purchases. For details, contact the publisher at the following address:

Epic Publishing
370 Castle Shannon Blvd., 10366
Pittsburgh, PA 15234

Or on the web at www.epic-publishing.com

To my biggest fan, my wife: thanks for being patient with me during the infancy of what I hope to be a long, fruitful career in making things up. You are the real MVP.

1

He was a horror writer. I should have known. Stories of sinister psychos and paranormal entities published twice a year for the last four decades, and I thought the guy was normal. I was wrong. I found that out the hard and painful way.

It began one Sunday morning in late May while I was rummaging through a box of used books at a garage sale a couple of miles north of the Grove City Outlet Mall near Slippery Rock, Pennsylvania. It was one of the larger hunts I'd been on, and more organized, too. The house was a modest-sized bungalow that had fallen into disrepair. Dandelions over a foot tall towered over the beige lawn. The front steps had decayed, the cement crumbling into piles of rubble that sat on top of floral skeletons in thirsty dirt. The roof looked like a chessboard, missing dark-brown shingles exposing tan rotted wood. The gravel driveway stretched fifty yards in from the road. Sitting behind a table at the foot of the garage was a pudgy man wearing a white T-shirt under denim overalls.

There was a continuous cycle of cars parking on and pulling away from the berm in front of the house, which was the last thing you wanted to see when approaching a sale. For one, there was something so gratifying about shooting the shit with the proprietor of a sale full of goods and short on people. You got to learn about the person, why they were having the sale, what was valuable to them, and, if you were lucky, they'd pull something "special" out for you, for sale, but not to the general public—only to "friends." I'm sure my dad had the same feeling when it was just him and the bartender. Enter a full bar? His heart sank momentarily as he assumed that it would take forever to get his order in, or worse, that they'd be out of his poison.

FINDERS BLEEDERS

At least twenty people were browsing through the clothesline with a rainbow of decades' worth of fashion, and I hated every one of them instantly. No kid likes when there are other kids hanging around an almost-busted piñata, and I saw people at sales as clueless gulls lurking for scraps. They weren't vultures, and maybe they weren't as ravenous as I was, but we were all there for the same reason: to find something we wanted. Seeing the crowd, I became increasingly paranoid, worried that anything of value was long gone, into the hands of somebody who, for whatever reason, didn't deserve it as much as I did. I rushed past the looky-loos and nearly shoved a young girl who was begging her mom to buy the plush bunny she'd found.

There were three long rows of boxes, all neatly labeled, from books and DVDs to socks and hats. Whenever there was a lot of stuff, I assumed somebody had died and it was time to get rid of the painful reminders. In a crude way, I think it was time to recoup some of that loss financially. If death turned a person's world upside down, then money helped to turn things right side up—or as right as they could be. Judging by the state of the property, though, I hoped that the proprietor might consider hiring a handyman or two.

I browsed through some of the random knickknack boxes, looking for bookends for my library shelves at home. I found none and moved on to the DVDs. *Road House*—a man's guilty pleasure and a woman's self-pleasure aid. At twenty-five cents, you couldn't go wrong. I tucked it under my arm and walked to the box of books. Whomever these books belonged to, they sure loved Evan Noble.

Not familiar with the name? He's single-handedly responsible for modern horror. He brought the genre out of the dark and made it cool. Not only can he write a million words a month, pumping out bestseller after bestseller, those books turning into Hollywood blockbusters that keep the kiddies up for weeks, but he listens to rock 'n' roll, plays guitar, and seems to know every minute detail about everything that has ever existed. The best part? He never came across as an asshole when spouting his genius. He seemed like a cool guy, talking about his main passions, passing on his sage wisdom.

There was everything in that box, from *Terry,* the story of a guy who enters puberty to discover he has the gift of mind control, to *Night Watch*, an amazing collection of short stories. I looked at the owner of the sale and wondered how nice it would be to jaw about our shared love for Noble. Being a huge fan of Noble myself, I owned almost all his stuff—everything, in fact, except for a copy of the post-apocalyptic epic *The Last*, which I'd lent to somebody and never gotten back. Remember Randy Flatts as the devil in that one? Horrifying.

I pulled *The Last* out from the bottom of the box, and before the neighboring books collapsed into the now vacant spot, I spied a small stack of paper with print on it, stapled at the corner. I exhumed the document carefully, like an archaeologist uncovering a thousand-year-old clay pot, removing the books that sat on top of it and piling them neatly on the concrete.

Taking the bound sheets out as carefully as you would bring a newborn into the world, I cradled the underside of the papers in both hands. There was a brown stain on the center of the title page, and the paper had yellowed from exposure to something—nicotine or sunlight, maybe. I didn't know exactly how old this baby was, but it felt timeworn and smelled like it had sat in a damp and dark room for too long.

It was a manuscript titled "The Murders in the Rue Morgue" by E. Noble. "**A R.I.B. Book**" was stamped in bold on the top right corner of the title page. It was about eight pages long, single-spaced, and printed on both sides of the page.

While I flipped through the manuscript, I couldn't help but feel as if I'd heard or read about this story somewhere. (I know Poe authored the original, but I mean this exact retelling.) I pushed away the inkling I had, chalking it up to nothing more than mistaken intuition. I continued to flip through it, but I couldn't ignore the whisper of a thought. I tried not to pay attention to the voice trying to validate my hunch—though it wasn't a *voice*, exactly. I'd have paid more attention to it. I'd have *heard* it. This was a prickling murmur of understanding, a thought standing last in a line of thoughts, waiting impatiently to be checked out at the register. I tucked the manuscript under my arm and continued to scan the other bins, my eyes returning to the box of Noble books.

E. Noble.

The mental lineup in my mind turned into an express checkout, and the last-in-line thought came rushing to the front.

"Jesus Christ!" I exclaimed.

Realizing that all eyes were on me, I blew out a puff of air and shook *Road House* in my hand as if it were the last copy in the world.

"This is my favorite movie, and I finally found it!" I nodded in agreement with myself and flipped the DVD around, studying the back for a synopsis I knew inside out, as if that would make me look less crazy and feel less embarrassed.

I was suddenly short of breath, my heart double-kicking. Holy shit. Holy shit. I just found a national treasure.

A couple of months earlier, I'd read Noble's *The Writ*, a memoir in which he details parts of his life, his writing habits, and his commandments for the craft. He even details being struck by a transport truck and getting hooked on painkillers as a result. Poor guy. He also talks about watching horror flicks with his friend and about how the one that had tickled him in the family spot the most was a film version of "The Murders in the Rue Morgue." He'd been so tickled, in fact, that he decided to do a novelization of the movie. He wrote and printed a whole bunch of them and sold them to his friends at school—*sold right out of them*. Talk about foreshadowing.

According to Noble, his retelling was printed on both sides of each paper, and on the top right corner of the title page, he had made sure to add his make-believe publication house in bold: **A R.I.B. Book**. *Just as Noble described it*, I thought. I was buzzing, at first from sheer excitement and then from anxiety. How did I know this was legit? How easy could it have been to replicate?

There was only one way to find out, and my appraiser would have the answer.

FINDERS BLEEDERS

I rushed toward the old man sitting in a lawn chair behind a plastic folding table he'd probably borrowed from a library or some veterans' organization. A sign that read "PAY HERE—CASH ONLY!!!!" was taped to the front of what was most likely the last desk this guy hoped to ever sit behind. Judging by the excessive exclamation points on the handmade sign, I figured this guy probably got the regular, "Do you take credit cards?" In this world, people undoubtedly still asked.

I handed him the DVD, the book, and the manuscript. He squinted, adding up the cost of the movie and the book, and then something changed when he got to the manuscript. He tilted his head down and peered through the top of his specs. For a brief moment, I heard my mind mutter about how this guy knew what the manuscript was and what it was potentially worth if it was authentic. Old Man Garage Sale was going to tell me to take a hike if I didn't want to pay a small ransom for the stack of papers, trying to take advantage of someone he'd taken for a fool for enjoying a good rummage.

Then I thought about how it had sat at the bottom of a box of books, and how it'd be the first thing to get soaked and destroyed in a flash flood, and how, if such a tragedy did befall such a grail in the holy world of literature, this wouldn't be the first box to be rescued. That'd be, of course, if he even gave enough of a shit to exert himself to salvage what he'd looked upon as third-rate garbage—valuable enough to sell for scraps rather than scrap altogether.

For someone who was undoubtedly in his late seventies, his forearms and biceps were thick and looked stronger than oak. He had a buzz cut and faded tattoos on both arms, proud reminders of where he'd been stationed in 'Nam, and maybe World War Two, and which battalion he'd belonged to.

"One dollar for the book, twenty-five cents for the flick, an'—" he studied the manuscript once more through his glasses, "—an' you can take the paper fuh free. That's . . ." He quickly mouthed the sum of the haul to himself. "A buck 'n' a quarter." He shot me a wink.

I gasped as if I'd been meandering through the Valley of the Shadow of "Huh?!" and someone had jumped out from behind a bush and yelled, "Boo!" I was so nervous. My ball sack shriveled up like a prune. It always happened to me before I got on a plane. *Calm down*, I told myself. *This could be a bust, is most likely a bust, so don't get your hopes up too high.*

"Thank you very much, sir," I managed to say. The pretense was crumbling, and even though I tried to be a pessimist and assume the worst, my body and mind ignored such caution and reacted as if I'd won the lottery. My heart was beating as if its time were running out, and I started to sweat. Clearly this guy had no clue what a pearl of a composition had sat in the depths of a box of his no more than a minute ago and was now conveniently in my left hand.

I felt as if I were holding a bomb, felt as scared as I'd imagine I'd feel if something *were* ticking in my palm, bound to detonate at any moment. I had to say something else to this man or *I* was going to explode. Nobody wanted to do business with a crackpot, least of all a vet who was getting rid of his personal belongings.

"Nice collection you've got here," I said. "Great books. Excellent movies." I held up *Road House*, still managing to hide my giddiness and apprehension.

He scoffed. "I've never read *his* books, an' I sure as hell haven't watched *that* movie. I prefer them Harlequin Presents books n'at, especially Lynne Graham's stuff. An' if it ain't got The Duke in it, I ain't watchin' it."

Ah. A man who enjoyed the finer things. If I were to stereotype a war vet, I'd say his movie collection consisted mostly of Steve McQueen, Charles Bronson, and, of course, "The Duke". So far, we were one for one. Harlequin Presents, though? *Really*? My mom used to devour those books, and when I asked her why she liked them so much, she said it was because the people and stories were so pathetic they made her happy. Different poisons for different 'poysons,' as she used to say. My dad would say that they were for queens and grannies with dried-up cunts.

The old man continued. "This is my

son's junk, anyway. That queen hasn't been back in five years an' ain't welcome back in this life n'at. I ain't gettin' any younger. At some point you gotta clean out the goddamned closet, even if that closet is a crawlspace an' it ain't your stuff."

Not knowing how to respond to such a personal confession from a total stranger, and acknowledging that the next word to come out of my mouth would be the explosion I'd been fearing, I handed him a five, turned around, and walked away, ignoring his pleas to collect the change.

I got in my car and burst out laughing. The bomb had detonated. I wasn't within earshot of the awkward yet pleasant old man, and I had my merchandise paid for. Signed, sealed, delivered—they were mine! Thank God for small favors. Blurting out the Son of God's name on a driveway packed with people and secondhand items was one thing; acting like I was in the process of getting away with the robbery of the century, nervous and skittish, was another. Someone would have thought something was up, and I'd have dropped my wares and hightailed it out of there. Maybe the old man would have thought I was on the reefer and not taken too kindly to my type. My type *and* queens, apparently. I'd take blasphemy over botching this garage sale find of a lifetime any day.

2

I headed south on 173 toward my home in Slippery Rock. Before getting into town, I stopped at St. Thomas Cemetery to say hi to Mom. I didn't have much to say so I blew her a kiss from the driver's seat and continued on.

I sped by Buck's Bar & Grille, where families *didn't* go to enjoy food, where few actually watched the Pirates, Penguins, and Steelers, and where most of the down-on-their-luck and hard-up-for-cash partook in that unspoken game of How Pathetic Can Your Life Get? Home of the barfly.

I was reminded of my dad, Mr. Pathetic, brother to another Pathetic, cousin to one more still—a rotten leaf on the

International Family Tree of Dipsoma-
niacs. I learned that word in therapy. It's
synonymous with "alcoholic," but it's
more accurate; they were a bunch of fucking maniacs. They'd wince with every sip
of J.D. or gag as they'd near the middle
of the bottle, cringing as they swallowed
what tasted like liquefied shit. There was
a cowardly machismo to being a man
who drank the hard stuff because it did
the job, all the while wishing to Jesus in
a manger that it tasted like cotton candy.
They weren't much worse than the ones
who *did* love it, and love it uncondition-
ally and at any cost. *Any* cost. They who
would pound the kitchen table to the beat
of Blind Lemon Jefferson's "Mosquito
Moan" and belt out "I love my whiskey
better than some people likes to eat," as if
it were the alcoholics' national anthem and
they were naïve patriots.

Dad.

I hated the asshole who thought that
his "friends" were the ones who sat next to
him at the bar, the ol' waterin' hole, sharing in each other's miserable excuse for an
existence ("Life can be so fuckin' cruel,

but at least I got'chu!"), patting each other on the back and toasting to their communal complacency for a shitty life.

Dad.

Then there was the inconsiderate alcoholic. The one with a wife and children. The breadwinner. The *man*. He was the one who gave mom shit for not bringing enough money home ("Do they even *pay* you at that fuckin' job?") yet blew a small fortune on the bottle and the bar.

Dad.

The problem with living in the small town you grew up in was that you knew where the haunted houses and ghosts were, but you still stopped and stared at them, like a rubbernecker trying to catch a glimpse of a corpse in a fatal car accident. The bad memories and forgotten faces never fully faded away. They couldn't. And part of you wouldn't let them. You also couldn't leave town because that was the easy way out. You needed to stay to prove to the people dressed in their Sunday best that you had defied the odds and survived without becoming what you were raised to be.

So I stayed. My place was on 435 Slippery Rock Road. Not very imaginative to live on a road named after the small town you live in, but people don't call it the simple life for nothing. The yellow dividing line of the two-lane road had long faded to a shade of black slightly lighter than the charcoal hue of the asphalt. During the day, you could tell the difference and stay on your side, but at night, if you weren't a frequent traveler of the area? Godspeed, lad. Once every five years or so, it was likely you'd wake up to the droning sound of a car horn, and you couldn't help but fear that there was a sixteen-year-old kid with his chest pressed against the steering wheel, the pulse in the horn instead of in his heart. Sometimes, the next day, you could find shards of windshield and scraps of fender or bumper swept to the side of the road—remnants of the previous night's head-on collision. They were apt to stay there for months, constant reminders of your mortality, until the wind carried them elsewhere or they sank into the mud of a farmer's field.

That was what my neighborhood

consisted of: farm fields and houses two hundred yards in from the road. Each property was about five acres. The ones that grew corn were up to fifty. On the east side of Slippery Rock Road were the barns and corn and hay fields. On the west were houses hidden behind elms that lined the road for miles at a time, standing at attention, shielding the houses from the tuneless hum of the utility poles and muffling the sound of passing cars. Private. Lonely.

Isolated.

Once south of town, and past the painful reminders, the drive home was relaxing. Nature had a calming effect, a tranquility you couldn't help but absorb. When I pulled up to my house, I put the car in park and sat idling for a few minutes, looking at the manuscript on the passenger's seat. Next to it, a cross-armed Patrick Swayze stared approvingly at me. I shut the engine off, grabbed my goods, and checked the stain of the table I'd been commissioned to refurbish. I also glanced over at my new mailbox, running my fingers over the engraved inscription RICHARD FAVREAU, which I'd just polished. Everything was drying nicely.

I opened the door to my house, a modest bungalow with two bedrooms, one bathroom, and a decent-sized kitchen and living room. The one guest who happened by whenever was my appraiser, Perry Dalton, and he always commented on the lack of family pictures. My reply was simple: my folks weren't keen on capturing moments in time. That usually made for an awkward moment of silence. My house was fairly bare, save for the bookcases in the living room, which were crammed with novels, CDs, and LPs, and the shelf in the kitchen, packed tight with cookbooks, several pages dog-eared to save my favorite recipes. I had what I needed, and anything else would have been excessive.

I took off my jacket, neatly squared away my new manuscript on the corner of the coffee table, and collapsed into the sofa with a copy of Evan Noble's latest book when the phone rang. I had a wild thought that it might be the old fart from the garage sale hollering at me that I'd ripped him off and needed to get those sheets of paper back before he had to find me and serve me up a fierce ass-kicking. An ember of panic flared in my chest.

I looked at the clock on the oven as it flashed 3:00 P.M. My anxiety turned into a mixture of annoyance and relief. It wasn't the guy from the garage sale.

3

On the Friday after the garage sale, I took the manuscript to Perry's antiques place in Butler, about fifteen miles south of Slippery Rock. I had taken plenty of rare finds to Perry before. He was the kind of guy who knew everything about everything—a wizard in the wonderful world of collectors. In the rare case he wasn't sure about the value or legitimacy of an item, he knew someone who would be. He was also a smug sonofabitch in his tweed blazers and colorful bowties, affecting a British accent when he talked even though he was born right here in Pennsylvania like me. He thought it made the big words he liked sound all the more educated. What it did was made him sound like a jagoff. But, he was thorough and, not to mention, the only appraiser within a fifty-mile radius, so I was somewhat stuck with him.

I told Perry where I had gotten the manuscript and had my copy of Noble's *The Writ* so he could read about some of the specifics of the document. He wrote some points down: "drum press, double-sided pages, A R.I.B. Book."

As he studied the manuscript, my fingers started tap-dancing on his glass countertop. After a minute, he looked up, first at my hands, then at me.

"It looks like you have a bona fide copy of one of Noble's first-ever printed stories." He added with a snide smile, "So far."

It was clear that something so special meant nothing to him, and he wasn't going to spare me his feelings now. He looked from his notes to the manuscript. "I am going to need a bit of time to compare the finer details—particulars like diction, syntax, and other stylistic devices. They have programs at the university that scan separate documents and compare similar-ities."

I mentioned that I thought I knew what he was talking about—the software that made sure students didn't plagiarize.

"Um . . . no. Not really," he said, seemingly annoyed. "Are you familiar with the author of those wizard books that have taken over the world?"

I asked him who wasn't. I didn't tell him that I thoroughly enjoyed them—both the books and the movies.

"Awful books, those." He shuddered. "Anyways, a few years ago, this mystery book came out, and a reporter got a tip that the author of that novel was also the author of the wizard stories and that she was using a pseudonym." His tone changed from aversion to a mild form of respect. "The author wanted to ensure that the literati lauded the work based on the quality and not the creator. So the reporter took some linguists to task. Rather than have them pore over different works by the same author, someone developed a Java program to do the hard work within minutes."

I nodded, surprised and interested. I hadn't known any of this.

Perry straightened up and fixed his bow tie. I felt like my ignorance was fueling his pomp. "They compared it with not only her work," he said, "but that of other authors in the mystery genre. Vocabulary, length, you name it, they compared it. Leopards do not change their spots, even decades anon. They published their findings that they were ninety-nine point ninety-nine percent certain that the author of the magic books was also the author of the mystery books. Then she came out and admitted it."

Perry paused for a moment. I wondered if he was waiting for a round of applause.

He continued. "Thus, that is what I will be doing with this work—running it through the same program at the university, comparing it with Noble's work and the work of his contemporaries in dark fiction. I will also have to dialogue with a colleague of mine about the physical properties of the document, such as the paper and ink, and, if it is possible, date them. I think it probably is, but I do not work with probabilities. I work with certainties. Do you write, Richard?"

I told him I didn't.

He laughed. "Consider yourself lucky. You see, writers mature, but they do not change, as perplexing as that may seem. A competent writer sheds his bad habits the way a crooked lawyer casts away a guilty conscience. He might change the mode of narration or tense, but his style stays unmodified. There are certain words and structures he has made his own. Every story he writes will contain analogous constructions, even if he tries his damnedest to change his style. Are you a fervent reader of Noble's?"

I chuckled at Perry's accidental reference to Noble's pet name for his loyal fans.

"What is so funny?" Perry asked.

I shook my head. "Nothing. In his epilogues, Noble directly refers to his faithful as 'fervent fictioners.'"

He motioned with a slight extension of his neck and held his palms up, signaling that he was impatiently waiting for the reply to his first question.

I cleared my throat. "Of course. I've read everything from *Terry* all the way up to the latest."

"Right," he said. "I cannot say I am a fan. Too dense and without purpose. Things that go bump in the night? Grow up." He cleared his throat and fiddled with his bow tie, adjusting it so that it was parallel to the floor.

I hated him more at that moment.

Perry continued. "Why do you keep reading Noble? Is it solely the stories or the genre? Or is there something else that keeps you revisiting?" He sounded mildly disgusted, as if he were a germophobe and we were talking about how I never washed my hands.

I thought about Perry's question for a moment. Noble's stories were great, and they were chilling. There were certainly times I'd left the night lamp on because I was scared shitless by something I'd just read. I think the lamp stayed on for the entirety of *Entity*.

"He writes people and places with so much detail, it's as if they're *real*," I said. "No doubt about it. I can picture everyone and everywhere in his stories, like there's a reel moving through a projector in my head." I was starting to get excited, as if I were talking to a friend in the schoolyard and describing my favorite toy.

But there was something else that drew me to Noble's stories. I reflected a little longer, Perry watching me closely as I searched my mind, hoping for a revelation.

And then it came.

"It's the way he writes everything! The stories are different, the characters change from book to book, but there is always something shared at the root. Like the way he, or the narrator—whatever— addresses the reader as 'pals and fellows.' It's in a lot of his stories."

Perry cleared his throat again. "That is his style. A plethora of characteristics can change from story to story, but there is always a trace of the writer. It cannot be helped."

Now I understood, regardless of Perry's ten-dollar words.

He seemed to notice my understanding and continued. "The phrases and other mechanics of writ are detectable through the scanning software. I shall compare what you have brought me with an assortment of other digital copies of Noble's literature, and we shall see what comes up. I will confer with my associate about the physical elements, and I will give you a call when I have an answer."

I said thanks, shook his hand, and turned toward the front door. As I pushed it open, Perry spoke from behind the counter.

"Richard? If this is Noble's, if I can verify it with absolute certainty, then you have one unwonted find on your hands. We are talking an immense amount of money. Fingers crossed." He held both hands up, crossing his fingers. He smiled, but it seemed as phony as his outfit and accent.

I smiled, held up my hands, and did the same.

Fingers fucking crossed.

4

Perry called me the next Thursday.

"It is definitely written by Noble," he said flatly. Was there a hint of jealousy in his tone? Annoyance? Like a pouting child folding his arms and staring at the ground because it wasn't his turn to use the tricycle.

He continued. "I ran the test against four of his texts, and the tense, diction, and—your favorite—'pals and fellows,' matched to a total of eighty-four percent. Compare that against the other dark fiction authors tested. The highest percentage of similarity was a meagre twenty-eight percent."

Excitement swelled through me. My

cheeks flushed like the coil of a stove burner. I started to feel my heart skip in my chest, the *thu-THUMP* banging on the walls of my neck and head.

He prattled on. "My colleague, Dennis Naughton, has a PhD in typography and the history of print. Obscure, I know, but he is a genius and has a passion for abstruse subjects."

Barf. He was the bearer of wonderful news so far, but the sound of his voice produced sour phlegm from the back of my throat. Did he even know how to define half the words he was using? Were they being used in the right context? I had no idea, but I would put my money on "negative."

"His analysis confirms the authenticity of the manuscript," Perry said. "The ink is from a typewriter that went wayward in the seventies, and there were also trace amounts of lead and mercury, both of which have not been used in ink since the early eighties due to the affordability of carbon black."

He took a deep breath and exhaled. "The manuscript is authentic. Noble

punched this very document. Congratu-
lations, Richard." His salutation held as
much delight as his sigh had.

Maybe he'd become possessive of my
document, or maybe he was suffering from
garage sale envy. I dismissed the idea. If
Perry Dalton developed feelings about
rare items that came through his store, he'd
have been out of business a long time ago.
He'd never struck me as the clingy high
school boyfriend of inanimate objects, and
he'd be caught dead before even dreaming
of rummaging through a garage sale. The
sun truly shone out of his ass.

I sat down on a chair at the kitchen
table, wiping sweat from my forehead and
running my hand through my hair.

When I said nothing, he asked, "You
all right, Richard?"

"Yeah, I'm good.," I finally replied.
"Thanks, Perry. I really appreciate all your
help. I'll swing by tomorrow and pick up
the document. What do I owe you?"

He didn't need to think about it.

"Three hundred dollars. I spent the
better part of six hours typing out the story
so I could analyze and compare the content

digitally. Not to mention the gas from here to the university."

Cheap bastard. I felt like reminding him that it was only a fifteen-minute drive to the university, and that the omission of his "colleague" from the list of services rendered suggested that he intended to pocket all the money. But I acknowledged help when I got it and was grateful. It'd be snowing in Satan's shower before I took on a task like the one Perry had.

"Sounds fair. I'll see you tomorrow. Take care, and thanks again."

"One more question, Richard," Perry interjected. "What exactly does 'R.I.B.' stand for in the title of the manuscript?"

"Reasonably Important Book," I answered, suppressing my impatience. I wanted to get off the phone.

He scoffed. "So, Noble's make-believe high school book imprint was 'A Reasonably Important Book . . . Book'? You have *got* to be kidding."

I shrugged, even though he couldn't see me. "I think we all did stupid shit back in high school, Perry. See you tomorrow!" I hung up the phone before he could snipe a reply, sat in the chair at the kitchen table, and beamed.

5

If a Sunday came around and it was pissing rain or the apocalypse was upon ye, I'd call off looking for garage sales, say a silent hello to my mom, and stay inside. Rain and the end of days are about the only things that can keep me from my treasure hunts. I have a favorite armchair that I like to hole up in on such days, and after breakfast, I read the paper and then a book. I usually have my folk music on, though I've been known to throw on some Beatles or Pink Floyd when the mood strikes. I have an affinity for grinnin' 'n' pickin' music. I'm a sucker for haunting melodies, hillbilly harmonies, and narratives.

If it's threatening thunder and lightning outside and the clouds are a menacing purple and gray, the air warm with electricity, I'm inclined to listen to Townes Van Zandt. If the day's miserable, "Play some tunes that fit the feeling," that's what I say. If the rain is sporadic and there's sunshine peeking through the light gray fog of early morning, I'll put on Roger Miller, maybe Dylan. Rock 'n' roll is for yard work and cooking, and it's written in my will that "A Day in the Life" be played throughout my wake.

I often thought of my mom on Sunday mornings.

Betty Favreau was a gentle woman who married Frank Tavis and birthed little old me. For the better part of a century, she worked as a cashier at Todd's Take-Away (a grocery store with a ridiculous moniker, in my opinion, because who bought groceries and left them at the store?).

She was a devout Christian, so it was her duty to drag me to church on Sunday mornings. I was about twelve years old when I started noticing my dad's absence. We were the only fatherless family in attendance, and my mom had to endure the snide comments and accusatory looks from the circle of "sinless" women and faithful parishioners after the service concluded.

"Poor Betty," they'd say. "A fool for marrying that Frank."

While everybody shook hands and exchanged face-saving pleasantries on the church steps—before they headed home to talk shit about the Wilsons' rust bucket of a car or how Ginger Gentry's earrings were most definitely not real pearls, and all of this prior to thanking God for a hot dinner and such a blessed day—we would scurry home like rats running from flood waters. The pity I felt in my stomach was worse than soda pop gut rot, because I knew she was embarrassed. *Humiliated* was more like it. You could see it in the way she stared at the ground as we walked home and hear it in the way her feet dragged on the rubble of the dirt road that led to our house. Mom looked like the town fool, because the man she'd married didn't give a good goddamn about us.

As a toddler, you heard whispers and

formed shaky opinions about things, like dreams that didn't make sense because they were filled with stories told in random order. Imagine tearing pages out of a book, mixing them together, and reading them. The words made sense, but the story didn't. Ten years later, you had a better understanding. You could *see* things and put the significance of it all together: a bare fridge and cupboards, hand-me-down clothes, and no hot water. And dozens upon dozens of empty bottles in the garage.

The bottle.

You knew your mom was at work, and you could bet your life that your dad wouldn't be home until you were asleep, and that he'd still be passed out when you woke up. You saw your mom crying while she cooked dinner and washed the dishes. You watched as she stood with her back to the kitchen counter, gnawing at her fingernails, taking momentary breaks to inhale her Marlboro Light, staring at nothing and nobody—the engine running but nobody behind the wheel.

That was when I started resenting my dad because I could read it on my mom:

he'd ruined her life. *Our* lives. Marrying my father was her biggest regret, she told me on her deathbed. But, she added, I was the sugar in her cold and stale coffee. I was worth all the shit she'd put up with—one of the only times I heard her swear.

And, oh, how I hated his two-strike rule.

One of my earliest memories is of him telling me to turn the volume down on the TV. "Strike one," he said when the volume remained the same. Before I could get off the couch to turn the knob left, he said, "Strike two," and jumped out of his chair. He grabbed me by the neck and twisted my earlobe until it was purple and hot with pain. He'd stop before what I always thought would be the point where my ear tore off. It didn't take long for me to learn how to keep to myself. I stayed in my room, poring over comics and books instead of sharing the TV in the living room.

My mom hated baseball, and for obvious reasons. If a meal wasn't cooked to his liking, strike two. If she didn't have enough of her hard-earned money to feed his habit, strike two. If she didn't want to have sex, strike two.

Strike fucking two.

Sunday had always dragged on for me, as it seemed to when you were forced to do something you hated. I enjoyed school because I had friends, and I liked learning. There was something sexy about knowledge. On Saturdays, I was allowed to hang out with friends, get in a little trouble, get dirty, laugh. Monday through Saturday, I was allowed to be a kid. Sundays meant church and having to see Mom downtrodden and weary and seeing my prick of a dad. That usually meant getting whupped for one thing or another.

As soon as I got out of that house for good, I went driving on Sundays to kill time. Garage sales helped occupy my time while I was driving around, and I became addicted to the search and the savings. There was rarely order to a garage sale's layout, other than they were always in the driveway and clothes went with clothes. You had to search to find something you liked. I always had a treasure map in my head, and it was exciting not knowing what today's "X" was going to be, or if I'd find the prize. It didn't hurt that digging through bin after bin in search of the day's find cost next to nothing. I think the most I spent at a sale was fifty bucks, and that was for a signed copy of one of John Lennon's biographies. Well, to be honest, it was signed by his son Sean, but it was still a valuable part of my library and a total win.

It was a child's game, really. As a kid, I was rarely afforded the opportunity to walk through the doors of a toy store and pick an item off the shelf. When it did happen, I remember being attracted to the bigger stuff first, then shifting to the aisles of the things that I liked—G.I. Joes, Star Wars figurines—and when I found something, the first thought that came to mind was, *Does anybody else have this? Will I be the only one?* It was like holding onto a secret that everyone else was dying to hear. I'd be flooded with a rush of excitement that, if I had been older, would have almost been sexual. Owning something, and, on top of that, owning something that was one of a kind, was euphoria.

Garage sales were the same. You were allowed the chance to take something away from somebody else while simultaneously satisfying yourself.

I drove around on Sundays in search of something new that might replace something old, slowly removing what was and starting fresh. Sometimes, though, you couldn't let go.

Two Sundays after I spoke to Perry, the forecast said that a hard rain was a-gonna fall. I glanced out my window to corroborate such a declaration and was disappointed to see a storm brewing to the east.

I made a coffee, sat down on my armchair in the living room, and started sifting through the *Pittsburgh Post-Gazette*. I usually read through the entire thing, but that day I was looking for something in particular. I got to the "local" section and found it.

"PA MAN FINDS RARE EVAN NOBLE TREASURE" was the headline.

The day after I spoke to Perry, I went down to his store and picked up my document. I gave him the money, we shook hands, and I started to turn away from the counter.

"Are you not going to enquire about the value?"

I almost forgot about it again. "I suppose I should, shouldn't I?"

Perry cleared his throat. "After calling my colleague again, we decided that a comfortable price would be in the eighty-thousand range. That's being conservative. We concur that, at the right auction, you could garner well over a hundred thousand." He had a cheap grin on his face, a swindler's smirk, and I couldn't help but feel that he wanted me to bow down and kiss the toes of his shoes.

"Right on," I said.

His wide-eyed excitement slowly turned into confused disappointment. Talk about an anticlimax. He scoffed. "You should be so lucky! Do you know what I'd do with a hundred thousand dollars?"

I thought, *Drink Moet and listen to Chopin until you start crying because even your mommy was ashamed of you?*

"It's not all about money, Perry. Thanks again and take care."

Here was a guy who was clearly envious of me, most likely praying I'd get side-swiped by a train while cross-ing the tracks on the way to his store, a hundred-thousand-dollar personal check behind his counter with his (and Noble's) name on it. But I had shown up, and he had tried to sell me the good news with his counterfeit smile.

The pang of envy I had sensed from him over the phone the day before was put into context. He was a dirty money-grub-ber who saw dollar signs instead of sentimental value. He'd sell his soul for a taste of how the other half roll and clearly didn't give a shit about the intrinsic value of anything. I turned heel and left him gaping after me.

***

On the following Monday, I got a call from some guy named Colin Lin who wrote articles for the "local" section of the *Pittsburgh Post-Gazette*. He informed me that a gentleman named Perry had contact-ed him about an extravagant find, and now Colin wanted to know if the tip was hot. I should have said no, but all I could think about was how Mr. Bow Tie had pulled one over on me and gotten the last laugh. With a grin on my face, I answered Colin, "Yep."

He drove out to my house on Tuesday afternoon to see the document and the certificate of authenticity. He recorded our conversation and asked how I'd found it, how I'd known what it was, and how much I was going to sell it for.

"Oh, I'm not going to sell it," I said.

Colin flinched. "Really? That's interesting. Most people would get an appraisal and put it on eBay or run to the nearest auction house."

"Yeah, I know there are people like that out there..." I cleared my throat and pictured Perry. I smiled. "... And that's fine. I'm a big fan of Noble's, and I just feel that it's something I'd rather keep than make a quick buck on. It's a cultural and literary treasure, and . . . I don't know . . . I feel that it'd be nice to own something so important. Look around. I live modestly and don't have much in the way of fancy and expensive ornaments. A small treat always caps off a final meal n'at."

A long silence passed. Colin studied me and nodded slowly, his lips pursed.

"Fair enough, man. Fair enough," he said. I could tell that the interview was over, and that he was having a hard time finding a segue to the conclusion. I started to get up to signal that we were done when he asked me another question.

"Richard, I forgot to ask. What do you do for a living?"

"I do woodworking n'at. Fix up old furniture. Guess I'm a bit of a cabinetmaker, too. Do the occasional fence, porch, and deck."

That was the extent of the interview. Colin thanked me for calling him and told me the story would most likely be published in the upcoming Sunday paper.

It was. I read the article, pleased that Colin hadn't misquoted me or given his opinion on the lunacy of not selling such a find. It was straight and to the point: I'd found it, it was worth this much, and I wasn't selling it.

At around 11:00 A.M., the first call came. The guy told me his name and asked if I was Richard Favreau from the paper. I said I was, and he offered me one hundred and fifty thousand dollars for the manuscript. I politely declined and hung up. My fingertips were humming. That was a lot of money.

Twenty minutes later, the phone rang again. This time it was WTAE-TV who wanted to interview me. I politely declined and hung up. Fifteen minutes later, there was another call with a lowball offer of ninety thousand dollars. I politely declined and hung up. Every two hours or so, someone would call. Sometimes they wouldn't talk; they'd just breathe into the phone and hang up, probably too timid to ask if I was the Noble-finder, Sir. Richard Favreau Esquire III—*now kiss my ring!* Receiver up, receiver down, over and over and over again. The only time I knew for sure that it wasn't someone trying to buy the manuscript was when the phone rang at 3:00 P.M. That was a whole other can of worms.

I politely declined and hung up on what must have been over a hundred people from Sunday to Tuesday. I avoided going to town for the week and hunkered down at home. By Wednesday, things had settled down.

Until Saturday, when Evan Noble knocked on my door.

6

Every once in a while, a Jehovah's Witness would knock and want to play Twenty Questions, even out here in the sticks. That was what I initially expected when I heard the knock at my door just as I was about to leave for some take-out.

I happened to look at the manuscript sitting on the side table in the living room before I opened the door. It dawned on me then that whoever was at the door was probably someone who'd read the article in the *Post-Gazette* and wanted to know if they could take it off my hands. I was kind of right.

When I opened the door, Mr. Noble, the creator of *Entity* and the Strollin' Fella in *Last*—the person who had dreamt up our worst fears and helped us confront them, grinned. He was taller than I had thought, but still lanky, almost hunched over. He was standing under my porch light, a crooked angel in black clothes, his hands behind his back, swaying to and fro, toe to heel.

"Richard Favreau?"

"Yes, that's me." This was a fucking dream. Why on a pagan's planet would *he* be at my front door, asking *my* name, instead of being at home in Vermont or Florida?

"Good," he said and flashed a sinister smile, his upper lip rolling up over his teeth. "I'd like my manuscript, if you'd please."

That was to the point. And I didn't want to, thanks.

He could be King Kong motioning that he wanted my banana *or else*, but if I wanted the banana, "Tough titty," cried the kitty. As a kid growing up with very little, what little I had now was mine to keep.

I was confused, though, as to why Evan Noble was on my doorstep, asking for my copy of his story as if it were a baseball card I had borrowed at lunch and forgotten to return. I shook off my bewilderment and answered him. "Uh . . . I'm sorry. I don't want to wedge your wishes or waste your time, but I won't be selling it to anybody. It's a keepsake of mine—a prized possession—and I intend to take it with me to my grave."

It was a bit of an awkward response, but random requests garnered graceless replies. I put my right hand on the door, the edge of it in the hook between my thumb and index.

He snorted, not breaking eye contact, still grinning like a madman and teetering back and forth. I was mildly amused by this. There was something hilariously unnerving about his facial features and the way he sounded. His voice was thin, and he enunciated every word with precision. His glasses were magnifying, his chin wide and his ears big. It all conjured up one word: nerd. *We recognize our own*, I thought. I fought the smile I felt forming and won. Yet his wardrobe and constant fidgeting made me nervous.

"Considering it's my story," he said, "I think it's only fair that I, the author of the work, be entrusted with its safekeeping."

They say you should never meet your hero because you're bound to be disappointed. I was slowly beginning to understand the credo. In my wildest dreams, I couldn't picture meeting Evan Noble and having our interaction be anything other than a fanboy session he'd had a thousand times. I'd say the same old things to him: "You're my favorite author. Where did you come up with the idea for Chu-Chu-Chosen? Did you like the movie adaptation with Corey Haim? I thought it was too much about the train and not the group of friends."

I snickered. "You wrote it forty years ago, or whenever, and sold it to your friends in high school for a quarter apiece."

"And I've plowed through yearbooks and Facebook for names and locations, and so far I've come up with shit. Nobody knows what happened with them. Some joked that they probably tossed them in the trash, maybe without reading it."

Noble's face hardened and his swaying hiccupped to a halt, as if a painful memory had suddenly sobered him up. "What a shame." He went back to rocking back and forth.

"I don't think you're in the right," I said. "You pissed away your ownership of it when you traded copies of it for cash. I happened to find what sounds like the only copy in existence, and I found it fair and square. It's like buying a book at a second-hand bookstore. The author doesn't see anything from the resale, but it's perfectly legal. I purchased this book from somebody who bought it before me. You have no legal or moral justification for standing at my front door, asking for *your* manuscript as if you'd lent it out to the world and have finally come to collect. You could offer me a million dollars for it, and the answer would still be no."

"I'm not offering you a penny," he said, grinning. "I'll ask one more time. Would you *please* give me my manuscript?"

I was starting to lose my patience with the guy responsible for redefining the horror genre in the twentieth century. My grip on the side of the door grew tighter in a subconscious defense. As my nervousness grew, he seemed to grow calmer. He stopped rocking back and forth.

"Well, we're clearly at odds, then," I said. "If you don't mind, I think we're finished here, so have a good night. I'm sorry you wasted your time." I started pushing the door closed.

He whipped his hands out from behind his back, revealing the shaft of a red baseball bat. He cocked his shoulder back and raised the club. I watched as the Red Sox logo on the shaft of the bat flew toward me. He brought it down on the arm I was using to lean against the wall next to the door, smashing my left wrist. I heard a crack and felt shards of bone explode halfway up my forearm. I screamed, recoiling into the hallway and cradling my arm. The pain slowly rose up my arm toward my shoulder, searing and torturous

How the fuck was he so fast and agile? Even my father at his best didn't have the cobra-like speed of Noble.

Behind me, the door closed and the

lock clicked into place. I watched him over my shoulder as he untied his black boots, slid them off, and placed them neatly in front of the shoe rack. He slithered across the floor in his black socks and brought the arm holding the bat over his shoulder again, looking like a demonic Yankee. My plea for him to stop fell on deaf ears. He stepped into his swing like a pro batter at the plate and connected with the back of my left knee. I felt my knee unhinge and dropped to the floor. The pain was agonizing, like having all your teeth drilled to the root without freezing or laughing gas. Hellfire and arctic freeze battled up and down my leg.

I tried to get up to run, but in my panic, I started on my injured leg. My knee buckled again, and I came down hard on my left arm. I felt something pierce my wrist and thought he had stabbed me. I let out a muffled scream, silenced by the gargling of my spit in my throat. I looked at my wrist and saw a piece of bone was sticking out like a cactus in the desert.

I turned onto my back, feeling the cold hardwood under me. My knee was jutting to the right, pointing inward toward my other leg. I started crying.

Noble stood over me, grim-faced and calm. He'd left whatever humor he'd been feeling at the door. He wasn't panting, hadn't even broken a sweat. He towered over me, his hands at his side, the bat with which he had effortlessly crippled me hanging gently against his healthy leg, a natural-born killer.

His clothes matched the part of a man accustomed to doing this sort of dirty business on a weekly basis—black leather jacket, black pants, black leather gloves—someone clad in clothing meant for dirty deeds. The devil incarnate.

He might not have done something like this before, but he'd created countless characters who'd done worse. He'd probably written and corrected every angle possible to ensure that all steps were covered and any missteps rectified. I realized he hadn't come over here on a whim. He'd looked me up, found out where I lived. There was likely a little black book in the glove box of his car with all of my info in it. Maybe this wasn't how he wanted the deal to go down, but I was certain that he'd thought about the *"what if"* of things going south. After all, he'd shown up hiding a fucking baseball bat behind his back.

"Please . . . please . . . st-stop . . ." I pleaded.

He just stood there and stared, studying me. His beady eyes glared at me from behind the thick lenses of his frames, looking like an owl hunting a mouse in a field.

I raised my right arm—I don't know— in a gesture of peace? Surrender?

He slapped my arm down. I watched the bat slice through the air. I felt a dull crunch in the left side of my head, heard a high-pitched ringing like a flat line on an ECG, and felt warm liquid run down the side of my leg.

And then it was goodnight, Coyote.

7

I was walking through a field of tall grass, my dad in the lead, holding a dark brown pump-action shotgun with a tan stock. We crept up to a clearing by the edge of a forest, each step a practice in silence. When we got to the edge of the clearing, my dad knelt, gestured to me to do the same, and pointed to a hole about twenty feet in front of us. I marveled at how much bigger he was than me. Even crouched down, he seemed like a giant.

He pumped the shotgun and handed it to me as if he were giving me a venomous snake. I looked at it for a moment, wanting to drop it on the ground and run away. But I tucked the stock into my shoulder and took aim at the hole, doing my best impression of a plastic toy soldier. Thirty seconds later, a pair of ears popped out of the hole, then a pair of sweet, wide eyes. We were a fair distance away, but I could see those innocent orbs clearly. The rest of the bunny hopped out and sniffed around, its whiskers trying to place the foreign and sour smell of sweat, cigarettes, and whiskey. I took a deep breath. My heart was in my throat. I choked back tears, knowing what happened when you pussed out. I had to be a man, and being a man meant pulling the trigger. The bunny leapt over a stick and stood in place again. I followed its movement through the sight.

"I'm sorry," I whispered, closed my eyes, and pulled the trigger.

The recoil threw me back five feet, twisting my knee and hurling me on my back. I landed in the mouth of the wild foliage behind me, dry stems biting into my back. My shoulder and knee throbbed. Dazed, I heard my dad yelping and looked to see him dancing around what looked like a fluffy snowball like a hillbilly at a hootenanny.

"You got the motherfucker! One shot!

A born natural, my fuckin' son! *Woo-hoo! Ha-ha-ha!* Now get off your ass and pick up your game!"

I got up, putting my finger in my ear to stop the ringing. I walked over and discovered that the snowball wasn't a snowball at all. My dad picked the rabbit up and held it out at arm's length like a fisherman showing off the day's catch. He extended his arm to me, presenting the unwanted gift, and I had an urge to say, "No, thank you." But I knew better. I took the bunny into my hands and cradled it. I wept. The carcass was littered with tiny holes, blood trickling out of each one like rust and calcium leaking out of a shower-head. I dropped the bunny on the ground, felt my knees start to wobble, and then the world went black.

8

A thump and the clinking of glass. A shout. No, not a shout. A sneeze, followed by another.

"Christ!" I heard Noble say. "Garage is like a damned sandbox!"

My eyes fluttered open, my kitchen warped in a hazy blur. Before the counter, fridge, and a shadowy figure came into focus, a random thought passed through my head: *Why would my dad make me hunt a rabbit with a shotgun? That's like fishing with dynamite.*

Another sneeze.

Noble was standing in my kitchen with his forearm held up to his nose. His free hand was gripping some sheets of paper. His eyes were squinting. He slowly drew in his breath.

The final sneeze.

"Goddammit!" he shouted and stamped with a sniffle. "What do you do in there, sand plywood, so you can simulate a desert?" He grabbed the dish towel hanging by the stove, blew his nose into it, then tucked the towel into his pants. "You got any pop? That's what you all call it around here, isn't it? Not cola. Not soda. Pop."

I shook my head, still dazed. How long had I been out? What had he been doing in the meantime? I drowsily looked around the room and then down to my feet. I was sitting in one of my kitchen chairs, turned away from the table, wads of duct tape wrapped around my wrists and ankles. There'd been nothing he could tie me to that had armrests, so he'd bound both wrists together and both ankles together. I felt like a fish. One wrong move, and I'd flop to the floor.

As the reality of what had happened set in, a foul stench came with it. I could see that my pants below the waist were drenched, and when I tried to move, I felt something warm and sludgy move between my legs. Although the pain in my wrist and knee was worse (both had been forced back into their natural positions after their earlier dislocations), the hot, wet texture of my own feces spreading around my cheeks and balls was somehow worse. The smell was putrid, the blend of piss and shit rising in successive waves. My mouth was taped shut, so I had no choice but to breathe through my nose. After a few whiffs, I started gagging. Noble ran toward me and ripped the duct tape off my mouth. He held the papers high in the air with his free hand. I caught a couple of words on the first page.

He had my manuscript.

"Not yet, big boy," he said. "Not like this."

I threw up again and again and again. I splattered his pants and socks on the first go-around and covered my floor on the next two. Just the twitch of my convulsion sprang new life into my wrist and knee, and it felt as if someone had slowly peeled away the skin and muscle and started hammering a nail into the naked bones.

He jumped backward, whipping my copy of his story behind his back. "*Goddammit*," he growled as he looked down at his puke-stained clothing. He stepped over the puddle of vomit, walked to the sink, and placed the manuscript on the counter, far away from the basin. He pulled out the semi-soiled dish towel from the waist of his pants, found the part that wasn't gooey, and wiped himself off.

My head was whirling. It felt as if a giant had my head clamped between his palms.

Noble turned my chair toward the kitchen table, walked back to the counter, slid the manuscript off of it and into his hand, and took his seat next to me.

"I'll leave your mouth free to yap," he said. "We don't want you to choke on your vomit. Not this minute, anyway." He seemed to be considering something, then pushed it away and shook his head. "However, if you try to sing the aria from your favorite opera, I'll slice your fucking throat from ear to ear. You get me?"

I nodded. My throat was on fire with acid, and every attempt to extinguish the burn with a swallow only fanned the flames. *I could use some antacids*, I found myself thinking.

"Grand," he said. "Now, I've read all about your find—the garage sale, the authenticating, even your refusal to sell or to allow another interview. Weren't quite expecting such a media show, were you?"

"No," I croaked. I cleared my throat, sour chunks of whatever I'd had for lunch rising onto my tongue. I chewed them and swallowed.

"No," he repeated, clicking his tongue and shaking his head. Was it pity or sarcasm? Maybe both. "Your phone must have been ringing off the hook with offers. What was the highest bid?" He leaned toward me, elbows on his knees, the manuscript held out between them, the title taunting me.

"One hundred and fifty thousand dollars," I said.

He pushed back into his chair and slapped his knee. "Woooooo! That's a lot of green, my man." He considered me for a moment, his beady eyes poking holes into mine. *"Are you crazy or just plain stupid?"*

he asked in his best Alabama drawl. He started flipping through "his" manuscript again, muttering, "One hundred and fifty thousand," over and over again, scanning the pages.

Without looking up, he said, "For *Terry*, I got two—"

"Two hundred thousand dollars," I finished. "Yeah, I know."

He met my eyes and did the De Niro—upper lip tucked into bottom lip, jaw pushed forward, chin raised—and nodded approvingly. "Not bad," he said.

"I read *The Writ* not too long ago," I explained. "I've read all your books."

"You're my number one fan, right?" He smiled. "It's been over fifty years since I've seen this relic. You know what's ironic? I thought about writing a story about all the kids at my school who bought copies of it. It would be about how there was a curse on each copy—not a curse I had pronounced, of course—and, at certain points in time, something bad would befall one of the owners of the copies. But that's where I got stuck—or distracted—and stopped."

He crossed his legs and started tapping his index finger on the table. He got up suddenly, and I flinched. He ignored my reaction and went to the sink. He took a glass out of the drying rack and filled it with water. Then he sat back down and asked if I wanted some water. I nodded, and he held the glass to my lips and tilted it. My throat burned as a wonderful chill flushed down my throat.

"Thanks," I said.

He gestured, *Don't worry about it; no problemo*, and gave me more water.

My fear hadn't disappeared completely; it had been replaced by confusion. Bound with duct tape at the points where action and reaction were possible, I was a prisoner in my own home. The guy who had taken a baseball bat to me three times was now casually chatting with me and giving me water. I was still scared, though not by what had already happened. It was the present that made me think this was the calm before the shit storm—the nice guy who bought the girl an expensive dinner and ended the evening by stabbing her fifty-five times because she said no to his advances. Some people don't take no for an answer.

Evan Noble sighed. "I still can't believe this has been found. I've actually spent a better part of my time between working on my novels—and even during writing and editing—scouring the Internet for the hack who beat me to the punch. I won't lie. I stopped at every garage or estate sale I passed with the small hope of finding exactly what you found." He got up and started pacing, hugging the manuscript to his chest.

He continued, talking to himself now. "Why couldn't it have been *I* who found it? I wouldn't have had to deal with this shit! Why couldn't it have been *anyone*— someone other than *you*, a rube all alone and hard-assed. Someone else. Anyone else, and surely, they would have taken an offer—not money but time. 'Come on in and have a beer, Evan. Is it okay if I call you Ev? Let's chat, and the manuscript is yours. Could I get a picture and an autograph, too? A photo op and your name scribbled down inside one of your novels puts your own fucking copy into your own fucking hands!'"

He stopped, his chest heaving as he blew out and sucked in breath through clenched teeth. He sat back down in front of me and addressed me.

"This is my intellectual property. Back in high school, I sold the stories under false assumptions. Yes, a transaction was made for cash, and goods were exchanged, but I didn't understand what I was selling. I was a kid."

I hesitated to respond, worried that I'd set him off again. I felt as if he wanted a response, though—a validation of his irrational behavior and outlook.

"You know what I did when I was a kid?" I said. "My friends dared me to take a shit in the public pool. I did it late at night, hanging from the lifeguard's chair. Next day was over a hundred degrees, and the pool was closed."

The skin on his forehead folded as he grimaced and recoiled.

"I'm not trying to be cute," I said, "but adolescent ignorance invalidates a deal you made? This isn't a contract you signed without legal representation we're talking about. You're not Tom Petty. Your logic is twisted. It's like saying you sold your car to some jagoff for five hundred, only to realize fifteen years later you could have gotten a thousand, so you chased him down and demanded he cough up what you thought you were entitled to. That's absolutely nuts!"

I expected him to lunge at me, but he only smiled.

"You're a smart cookie," he said. "Agree to disagree. The manuscript is mine, and you forced me to do this to get it."

I laughed. Not scoffed. Not choked on phlegm the way you do when you're surprised by something someone said. I barked laughter and did nothing to suppress it. The convulsions brought that hammer back down on my wrist and knee, but I couldn't help but laugh through the agony.

"I *forced* you? I didn't put you in my front door. I didn't put a bat in your hand. I didn't make you use it. And I didn't make you make me sit in a pile of my own shit and piss! So fuck you, Evan. I may have blinders on when it comes to going

70

to garage sales, and I may be very selfish about the whole experience, but you've gone completely fucking insane. Think about it. You attacked me and crippled me for a manuscript *A manuscript*. I didn't buy your wife or any of your kids. I didn't buy your fucking dog, for Christ's sake." I was whispering now. "A manuscript, man."

His smile was gone. He seemed to be taking my point into careful consideration. "It was *my* manuscript," he said simply. It was as if there had been no exchange at all. He was calm and collected again. Unburdened. At peace.

He turned away from me, still hugging the manuscript, and then turned back around. He sat down at the table, nestled his chair closer to mine, and laid the manuscript out on the table. He started flattening it out, running his finger down the creases on the front page, trying to scrape off the yellow-brown stain with his manicured fingernail, and then pushed the document away from him without removing his fingertip from it.

We sat in silence for a few minutes, and I got to thinking. Noble had knocked on my front door just after 6:00 P.M., and the time on the stove clock now read 8:13 P.M. It had been over two hours since I was beaten unconscious—two hours that I'd survived. I'd been playing nice, and now he was, too. A ridiculous notion crossed my mind and stuck. Maybe I could befriend him, persuade him into believing that I wouldn't go to the cops. I wouldn't even ask for help with the medical bill. I'd heal up eventually, and I'd be tight-lipped about tonight until the day I died.

However, there were still two issues: the baseball bat and the manuscript. He had brought over a weapon thinking he might have to use it. If he used it, he'd have to finish the job. Nothing else made sense. I had denied Noble's initial request that I hand the manuscript over to him, and he had attacked me as a result. Not really a punishment-fits-the-crime sort of thing, but it had happened, and I was the one hog-tied in my kitchen. He wasn't leaving here without "his" manuscript. And even as I sat bound together in a pile of my shit and a puddle of my piss with a broken leg and shattered wrist grotesquely repositioned by an author rather than a doctor, I briefly entertained the idea that he might let me walk.

And sure, it was only a manuscript. I got that. But I wasn't losing this time. I'd been a loser my whole life, raised by a woman who was stuck with a life that made her life miserable, and abandoned by another loser who drank his life away and beat on his family. I didn't have friends. People disappointed. I had *things*. I loved what I owned because things didn't tell you that you were worthless or take a belt to your ass or throw an empty bottle at your head. They didn't leave you to fend for yourself in a world where the weak were like mice to the hawks circling over them.

Things didn't break your heart.

I didn't hoard, but I didn't let go that easily, either. I collected. What was mine was mine. Whether it was worth one penny or a lot of pennies, if I wanted to keep it, then keep it I would.

But the optimism was short-lived. I found myself returning to my original belief that I was fucked and had been since

I'd said no. The damage was more than done. For a moment, it had felt like there was nothing left to lose.

I wanted to *live*. At the intersection of Favreau and Noble, I stalled.

"For that story you started to write," I began, "y'know, about the cursed copies of your book?"

Noble was at the kitchen counter, washing the glass I had drunk from. He asked, "Yeah, what about it?"

"Well, based on what you've told me, I think you have enough for a short story, or maybe even a novella." While his back was to me, I started looking for something, *anything*, that I could grab and use to cut my hands free. The counters were bare. I couldn't walk, so cupboards and drawers were out of the question.

He turned around and leaned back on the counter, flapping his hands in the air to dry them. "Really? What's that?"

"Let's say there're twenty kids who bought copies," I said. "As they grow up and move on, bad things start to happen to some of them. One gets hit by a truck, another gets struck by lightning, so on and so forth. One of the kids becomes a recluse, y'know? No friends, no family. He sits inside all day and reads the paper and books and lives on canned pastas and bologna sandwiches. As he reads certain papers at certain points in time, he starts to piece together that these are all the kids he went to school with."

Noble walked over to the table, sat down, crossed his legs, and folded his arms over his chest.

I continued. "So, he does some digging. Somehow, he discovers it's the story they bought from you, and somehow he figures out that the copies need to be destroyed—all of your classmates do—in order to end the curse."

He smirked and shrugged.

"There are definitely some parts that could work," Noble said. "I like that the onus is on the one character to break the spell. But why is he a hermit? Why him and not the others? And why does he piece it together? How does he know that the copies need to be destroyed? Does the story take place over twenty years so that he can see if his theory worked or not, or are there rules and specific times for the curse?"

I figured he was asking himself more than he was asking me, but then he stood up, staring at me, and I suspected that he wanted me to answer each and every one.

"I don't know," I said. "Nothing comes to mind. Besides, it's *your* story. I'm just trying to help you uncover the fossil."

He grinned, acknowledging yet another reference to his work.

There was something else I wanted to add, but to say it meant possibly triggering another violent bout: the antagonist could be a deranged author willing to do what it took to get his hands on "his" property.

"Touché," he said. "Do you have anything to drink besides water and milk?"

"Yeah. I've got some pop in the garage, through the door, beside the washroom." I jerked my head in the direction of the door. That hurt.

He walked across the kitchen and through the door into the garage. As soon as the door closed behind him, I started my second search for whatever could free me.

I tried to stand up and look in the living room, but I fell on the table and back into my chair as soon as I put weight on my leg. Thankfully, nothing had clinked or made enough noise to raise suspicion. Hopping to the knife drawer was out of the question, as was flopping and wiggling across the floor—at least for now.

He came back into the kitchen, pop in hand, pulled his chair closer to mine, and sat.

"Listen," he said. "I'm damn near exhausted. I didn't know what to expect coming over tonight, but I supposed something like this was a remote possibility. I didn't think beyond that, which is why the 'Great Thinker' is stuck with a bit of his thumb up his ass. Frankly, I don't know what I'm going to do with you. Frankly again, I don't see how I can walk away from this knowing you're alive. I'd wake up every day and think, 'Is this the day that lucky prick from Pennsylvania whom I let live is going to call me and blackmail me or turn me in?' Not likely.

"But, I'm not set on that just yet. So, I'm gonna sleep on it. And you're gonna stay right where you are. I'm not carrying you to your room, and you're not sleeping anywhere near me. I'm sorry you shit yourself, but bad smells spawn bad dreams, and I'd like to sleep peacefully and have a clear head to think with tomorrow."

He got up and carried his drink and *my* manuscript toward the living room. He stopped in the doorway and turned around. "And just in case you plan on being adventurous during the middle of the night, I took your knives and sharp objects out of the drawers while you were knocked out, so please don't waste your time or mine by trying to rescue yourself. Goodnight." He disappeared into the living room.

Had he really taken the knives, scissors, forks, and can opener away? Maybe he had and maybe he hadn't. If he had, that was the ball game. Noble with the shutout. If he hadn't, how could I possibly get to the drawers? I could shimmy in my chair, but I'd get no more than two shifts in before Noble woke up and I was retired for the rest of eternity.

My back was aching, and my ass was numb from the wooden seat. My splintered and shifted wrist was thumping in sync with my heart, each pulse a shard of pain driven up and down my arm. I bit the flesh below my lower lip to manage the pain. It felt as if someone were lifting up the tendons in my knee and letting them go, snapping them like elastic bands, each retraction a new searing throb. I didn't think I could sleep this way, but I rested my head against the shelf behind me—the one holding the cookbooks and mail—and fell into a dreamless sleep almost instantly.

9

When I woke up, I immediately thought I'd fucked up. I'd wanted to stay up until I knew Noble was asleep (*Does he sleep?*) and take one more stab at finding something I could use to free my wrists and ankles so I could at least die with some resistance and dignity.

Dignity. Heh. I guess there was little dignity left to lose and none to gain when you were up to your ass and around the corner in your own shit and bound at the extremities like a lassoed cow.

The clock on the stove read 11:50 A.M. How I'd slept upright in a cheap chair for over twelve hours was a bigger mystery than the Bermuda Triangle, but it had happened. How Noble had slept as long was clear. He was pushing seventy and had expended a week's worth of energy beating me. Add his mental exhaustion—considering what he was going to do with me, how he was going to do away with me, or (pretty please with sugar on top) whether he, without fear of retaliation, would let me live—and we were talking about a very tired boy. I was sure he'd have slept for a full day if he could've, but the man had written plots in which characters were trapped. Common sense told you the longer someone had to figure out an escape, the more likely it was they would.

The back of my head felt like it had been dented from sleeping with my head on the shelf. The left side of my neck was sore as if I had slept by an open window with a cool draft. But those maladies were small fries compared to how my wrist and knee felt. With every passing chunk of time—sleep, a conversation—the pounding had only intensified. At this point, I'd have been okay with parting with those limbs forever if it meant the pain would stop.

I turned my head to the right and looked again for a knife, saw, or hatchet that had grown a pair of legs and jumped on the kitchen counter to rest. Maybe Noble had put one there for me, an early Christmas present, a double-dog dare to fight.

Nothing.

I turned to the left, wincing at the pain in my neck. I had to turn my entire body to the left while holding my neck straight. My wrist and knee were not happy.

Nothing.

There were still the drawers, the sink, and the dish rack. Noble had probably told the truth when he said he'd removed anything that would aid in my escape, but what if he was bluffing? If I could slide out of the chair quietly and drag myself to the knife drawer . . . No, that wouldn't work. A delusion of grandeur; that's what that was. Have you ever heard of a baby surviving a three-story fall and thought, *Big deal*? It was because you had no comprehension of what your body could (and couldn't) handle. The reality was that if you hit concrete from three stories high, your hips would sink into your ribcage, your knees would drive into your hips, and your shins would drill into your ankles. And that was if you landed on your feet. Either way, it'd be Goodnight, Coyote.

But stranger things had happened, so what if I *could* manage to let myself off the chair lightly? I could turn around, put my weight on my good hand, and start sliding, resting my stomach and chest on the edge of the seat until my legs and ass were on the floor. No knife? No problem. I could crawl like an inchworm to the dish by the front door where my car keys were and slink out of the door and through the trenches, as it were, to my car. I probably couldn't drive, but I could put the car in reverse, step on the gas, and hope to God that I'd crash on Slippery Rock Road, right in front of a passerby.

I'd be saved.

I'd also have to be dumber than a wicker basket full of water to think that Noble wouldn't hear me before I got to the door or opened it. The jingle of my key chain would do the—

The keys.

They weren't in a dish near the front door because I'd gotten rid of the stand a couple months ago. It had taken up too much space in the hallway and I was always banging my hip on it. The keys were now on the shelf in the kitchen—in the *Goonies* dish.

I turned around as gingerly as I could, keeping in mind that everything would go to shit if Noble woke up. Right under the Emeril Lagasse and Jamie Oliver cookbooks, on the bottom shelf, was the key bowl. Inside the dish was nothing but a parking ticket I'd gotten three months earlier that I was going to take to court—not even a fucking pack of matches to light and scar Noble with before he finished the job.

Before I could embrace the dread that was about to wrap its arms around me and squeeze, I heard Noble cough and sniffle. The leather couch crunched with his wakening. Although I couldn't see him, I could hear the grating of the stubble on his face as he ran his hands over his chin and cheeks. He cleared his throat and farted.

In one final attempt, hoping and praying to a god I had long ago stopped caring about and turning to, I scanned the shelf where the keys should have been—CDs, a Pirates postcard, unfolded utility bills, and some letters.

And then I saw the letter opener.

It was about four inches long and looked like a mini Excalibur. The blade was dull, but the point was very sharp since I had never used it—or even known I *had* it.

I didn't have time to scold myself for forgetting that the letter opener had been right behind me the whole time because Noble got up off the couch and started dragging his feet toward the kitchen. I reached up and grabbed the letter opener, banging my left knee as I turned and extended my arms. I bit down on my lip to stifle the cry I wanted to let out, turned around, and held the blade in my lap, a metal erection in my limp wrist Noble would frown upon if he saw. I stood up an inch off the chair and hid the sword by sliding it flat under my ass, biting down on my lip again to fight the savage pain in my knee, which felt as if its bones were slowly being crushed by the turn of a clasp. White specks started flickering and fluttering around the room.

I slumped in the chair when Noble came into the kitchen. He put the manuscript down on the counter, then dragged his palm across the front page until his hand slipped off.

"Good afternoon," he said with a smile-nod. "Your lip's bleeding."

I licked my lips and swallowed down the liquid copper.

"Good afternoon," I said. "That was quite a nap you had." He was putting on a pot of coffee.

"I feel like I got into a fistfight with a mountain," he said, his back to me, watching the coffee drip into the pot. He rotated his shoulders forward and then craned his neck to each side. "Damn, I need to do more exercise than a daily walk." He walked over to the fridge and studied the contents, then removed eggs, bacon, onions, and tomatoes. He put everything on the counter next to the sink and returned to the coffee. He poured two cups and asked how I took mine. After I told him, he prepared them, brought the cups to the table, and sat down. He took a sip first, releasing a satisfied "Ahhh," before smacking his lips. Then he took my cup in his hands and started to raise it to my lips.

"It's all right. I can do it," I said.

He shrugged and put my cup back on the table.

I picked it up, using as much of my right hand as I could, the cup shaking, and took a sip. The warmth sank down my throat and into my chest and stomach, like electricity returning in the middle of the night after an outage. Goddamn, that felt good. It even seemed to wax over my injuries a little.

He smiled and moved his chair closer to mine. Looking me in the yes, he asked, "Do you watch baseball, Richard?"

"No," I said. "Baseball is just a bunch of old men scratching their crotches and chewing tobacco n'at."

He laughed. "It's so much more than *n'at*! It's a game of strategy, of probabilities and proper matchups based on analytics. It's like chess!"

"It's an inactive sport," I said, "a contradiction of the very term 'sport.' It's the only sport where fat people are paid millions of dollars to do nothing but hit a ball four times a game. Did you know that baseball players who bat a thirty-percent average are considered good? If they bat thirty percent, they're doing their job. Imagine that. You write thirty percent of a story and your publisher slaps you on the ass and says, 'Good job, kid,' and then scrapes the itch from his groin. It's lazy. I'd rather watch rugby, even though I don't understand it. No, I'd rather watch *cricket*! At least *something* is happening."

Noble did the De Niro again. "You know your sports. And what sports do *you* watch, Richard?"

"Hockey," I said proudly.

"Ah, a Canadian's game. Suppose you like the Pens?"

"Yup. And the Canadiens. Watched them a lot as a kid."

"Sidney Crosby," Noble said. "The world's biggest crybaby."

I smiled. Everybody always said the same thing about Sid. "He cries while he buries your team at clutch moments and raises the Stanley Cup."

Noble laughed again. "I can see by your collection that you're into music. You're missing Springsteen."

"He sucks," I said, looking past him and to my records on the back wall of the living room.

Noble twisted his face. "He's the all-American working-class musician. He revived rock 'n' roll."

I soured my face. "When a record label promotes the new guy as the next Dylan, that guy has a lot to live up to and a whole lot of room to fall hard. Springsteen fell. You can't even compare one to the other."

"*They say vanity got the best of him . . .*" Noble crooned, then shrugged. He looked over to the counter—to the manuscript. Then he returned his focus to me, wearing a grin. "You've got quite a library. Not as vast as mine, but I'm glad you read. Keeps people like me in business."

I laughed, despite my situation. It was a funny thing to say.

He went on. "Fascinating stuff. I scanned through a couple of your other texts. Woke up in the middle of the night

J. DONNAIT

and couldn't get back to sleep right away. *Trains of the 20th Century*? *Gardening During Christmas*? Why on earth would you have *those*? You don't strike me as a train guy."

"I'm not," I said, slightly annoyed. I couldn't imagine some of the junk I'd find in *his* library. "I got them as bookends. As you can see, no trains and no garden."

"Garage sale?" he asked.

"A buck a piece. Couldn't find bookends that cheap anywhere."

He laughed softly and took a sip of his coffee. "You've got a decent horror collection. Which is your favorite?"

"Bradbury's The October Country."

"Ugh! *Love* that one!" he exclaimed. "Best story in it?"

Easy answer. "'The Man Upstairs.'"

He slammed his hand down on the table. "*Yes*! The stained glass window? Shit, what a treasure that man was." He looked at me for a few seconds as I nodded. "You have all my work." He shot a glance at the counter again. "Emphasis on '*all*.'"

"Everything except for *The Upright*. I let a friend borrow it and never saw it again."

90

"Ah," he said sympathetically. "I hate when that happens."

I continued as if I didn't hear him. "Until very recently, I was a big fan of yours," I said. "Rushed to the bookstore whenever a new one came out."

Noble frowned sarcastically. "Sorry about that. I notice you don't really have any of the grandmasters, like Lovecraft."

I shrugged. "What's to love? I respect the contribution to the genre n'at, but I can't read that old stuff for the same reason I can't watch silent films—too outdated. I was raised on a certain language without a love for anything older. Chaucer's work may as well be in Greek."

"Yeah, it takes some time to get into the classic tales," he said. "Read enough of them, and it starts to become easier, like learning simple equations as a kid. That's how it was for me, anyway. I devoured that stuff when I was knee-high on my mother. What do you think about my son John's work?"

"Talent obviously runs in the family," I said flatly. I was starting to get irritated. I thought, *Why does he care? What's it to him whether I like Lovecraft or John Knoll?* I began to feel like Hansel in the witch's cottage. I was being primed, coddled, so I wouldn't fight when the time came to get roasted.

I was caught in a weird place. The events of the last twenty-four hours had been beyond surreal, and with the bizarre had come the notion that this couldn't be real, even though I knew it was. My limp wrist and swollen knee were proof of how real things were. Yet with the sense that things were too strange to be true had come a false sense of empowerment, that even though I knew this was all happening, I could afford to say what I wanted without consequences, because we had both entered a land where anything went. However, I needed to delay him, which meant keeping my mouth shut as much as possible. I had told him he couldn't have "his" manuscript, and he'd clubbed me; imagine how he'd react if I told him I thought *Necessary Objects* could be read to patients in need of sedation? That book could have been used as a headstone— that's how big that doorstopper was. It was almost a thousand pages of sinister schemes to the point that it was a story about setting up a story about setting up a story. It was maddening.

I decided that I needed to keep him talking. Maybe I could prove to him that I wasn't an object, something that could be switched off or pressed between bound pages.

I was about to open my mouth to ask him what his favorite horror movie was, but before I could part my lips, he whipped his head toward the time on the oven. He stood up, walked toward the sink, and mumbled something to himself. I thought I heard him say, "This is all useless," but I wasn't sure.

"What?" I asked.

He walked over to *my* manuscript, put his hand down on it, and closed his eyes. Then he turned around, his smile melted away, and his eyes narrowed. (Somehow, they could get even smaller.)

10

He sat down and stared into his coffee. "I've determined that I have no choice but to kill you.," he said. He took a sip, keeping the cup in his hand, and looked up at me. "I don't want to. That, you can believe, kid. I know I'm going to struggle with it at first—hell, maybe *forever*—but I've got too much to lose. I have a wife, children, and grandchildren. A corgi that destroys my couches. I love my life too much to risk you fucking it up by deciding you want your revenge on me—and trust me, you would wake up one day and decide that it was time for payback. It's human nature to not want to lose."

He took another sip, looking back over his shoulder at *my* manuscript.

"I also know that your death would never come back to me. First of all, you don't have family or friends. There's not even one picture of anybody you know. Look around. This place is the epitome of 'single and not looking.' You've got a million tacky knickknacks all over the place, no doubt finds from a garage sale or seventy. Your contact with people is scarce—I brushed up on you a little before I came here. Quite a nifty carpenter, apparently. Google is a wonderful voyeur tool. How many people would need to call about fixing their deck railing or the bottom stair before they asked about where you'd disappeared to? Maybe someone would think about coming here to check on you then. Doubtful, but possible. That would give me a while before somebody discovered your body. I'd make sure it would be as if I had never been here. I think I know how to clean a place up."

He raised the cup to his lips, considered something for a moment, then brought it back down.

"I'd take the manuscript and secure it somewhere nobody knows about—not even Babs," he said. "Everyone has at least one secret. Nobody would ever know I had it except me. And that's the kicker, Richard! The police would know the manuscript was missing. You had your fifteen minutes of fame a couple weeks ago, and any news in a small town is *big* news. They'd search the house for DNA and wouldn't find any. They'd ask your neighbors if they'd heard or seen anything, and of course, they hadn't. You can't see the road from your porch, for crying out loud. They'd keep an eye on the Internet for a copy of Evan Noble's "The Murders in the Rue Morgue," but it'd never surface. Your murder would become a mystery, a distant memory, a cold case file, and then history."

He took another sip of his coffee, never breaking eye contact.

What could I say? He was pretty much right. Anybody who really wanted the manuscript could have shown up to take it. Noble had all the time in the world to clean this place top to bottom, and like he said, he knew what he was doing.

"Well, I guess that's it then, isn't it?"

I said.

But that *wasn't* it. I wasn't dead yet, and I'd make sure that I went down swinging. Well, maybe not *swinging*, but not without a struggle. I was sitting on an ace, and I'd find an opportunity to use it.

Noble gave a sympathetic smile. "If you want, after breakfast, I can help you take a bath. I wouldn't want you entering heaven with a brown stain on your pants. If the coroner has to clean your shit up, word will get around town, and you'll be remembered by some cruel nickname."

I thought about informing him that the recently deceased generally loosed their bowels, and the coroner has to clean them up regardless, but then he got up to make us breakfast—not before returning to "his" manuscript to run his fingers over it again.

He made an omelet with onions and tomatoes and a dozen strips of bacon. I thought about taking my time to eat, delaying the end that was approaching. But when he placed the plate in front of me, fluffed the omelet, and turned over the bacon, my stomach grumbled. Seeing the food was like finding a river in the desert after days without water.

He fed me, shoveling mounds into my mouth and grinning, as if he were enjoying it, remembering the days when his kids were tots and he had to fly the spoon plane into their mouths. We each devoured a hungry man's portion, like starved pigs in front of a full trough. He cleaned up, did the dishes, and made more coffee.

"All right," he said. "Let's get you into the bathtub and get this over with."

I started to fidget with my fingers, caught myself, and stopped.

"If it's all the same to you," I said, "I'd like to skip the shower in favor of something else."

"Something else, huh?" he repeated. "And what would that be?"

"First of all, it's going to be hell to clean up, and I can't do it. Are you willing to rinse shit and piss off me—shit and piss that has dried and crusted n'at? Probably not, Scott. You'd have to carry me to the tub and then dress me again. That means you'd have to unbind me. And I think someone as careful as you wouldn't risk freeing me, even momentarily and with a baseball bat in hand. The whole affair would be more uncomfortable than sitting here and exiting stage left sitting on hard shit. I'm in fucking pain, and if you don't mind, I'd like to stay right where I am.

"Secondly, while the meal you cooked up was delicious, it's not exactly what I'd consider a 'final meal.' Since I'm an inmate of Noble Penitentiary and sitting on death row, in lieu of a proper final meal, I'd like you to read one of my favorite short stories of yours. I want to hear you tell me the story from beginning to end. After that, you can do what you need to do." Noble was looking at me like I was the one who'd lost his mind rather than the other way around. "Yes, you heard me right, so stop looking at me like that. Did you expect me to cry and beg for my life? Your earlier deduction was correct. I'm a lonely person without family or friends, and after a few weeks, I'd be an after-thought even to the police. It is what it is. I've accepted what you're going to do, but the question is, can *you* accept it and live with it? I don't give a shit.

"So, do me a favor. Grant me my wish, genie. Let me enjoy the last few hours I have the way I want. I've always been a huge fan of yours, and despite what you've done to me and what you're going to do, I want nothing more than to be read a good story by a great author. Can you do that for me?"

He sat eyeing me for a few moments. He might have expected a lot of things—defenses, pleas, and scorn—but not acceptance, honesty, and compliments.

"Uh—" he began, then cleared his throat. "Yes, that sounds fair." He took a sip of his coffee. He got up and walked toward the sink, forgetting to touch or look at *my* manuscript, then turned around. "Which story did you want me to read?"

I told him I wanted to read "A Confined Spot" from *Shortly Before Night*. It's a story about a guy who gets trapped in a portable toilet by a neighbor who wants him dead. The guy escapes, covered in human waste, and exacts revenge on his nemesis. The best part is that the guy doesn't kill his enemy; he scares the shit out of him and lets him die slowly from the cancer that is ravaging his body. Only the bad guy shoots himself a couple of days later, no doubt humiliated, tired, and scared. It was one of my favorite short stories by Noble, but now I saw the correlation between my situation and the protagonist's. Perhaps, subconsciously, I had chosen to hear that story for inspiration—never-give-up and bide-your-time type of shit. Maybe I had chosen it because it was a good one to hear before you died—a "last story."

Noble poured us some more coffee, picked the book up from the bookshelf in the living room, flipped toward the end, and found the first page of the story. Before he started, he chuckled. "I'm sorry," he said. "It's just funny."

"What is?" I asked, smiling as his body convulsed with giggles.

"I got the idea for this story when I was using a roadside toilet. When you're in one, you can't help but feel claustrophobic, thinking about what else besides piss, shit, and puke is down in that hole. Or how you scan the top corners for spiders or bees. How you spend the entire time scared and want to get outta there as fast as possible." He shuddered. "Do they creep you out that way, too?"

I told him they did, that I had to hold my breath before entering and couldn't breathe until I left, pushing the door open and gasping for fresh air.

He nodded. "Right, and that's when I thought about how terrifying it would be to be trapped in one that was tipped over on its door. Anyway, I was laughing because you smell about as bad as a portable toilet at the end of an exceptionally hot summer. And, well, the subject of the story you want to hear. It's just too much."

I told him I'd had the same thought, and we both smiled.

The time on the stove clock read 1:14 P.M.

He read the story with passion, enunciating the words with a poetic cadence. I closed my eyes and watched as the scenes played in my mind, interrupted occasionally by the pang of searing heat in my twisted joints. The damn pain couldn't make up its mind, and I found myself distracted, anticipating the next jolt and what new sensation would come with it.

FINDERS BLEEDERS

At 3:00 P.M. on the dot, just as Kirk Davidson escaped from the potty, my phone rang. Both of us jumped.

"Do you know who it is?" Noble asked.

"No clue," I said. "I get a lot of those sweepstakes calls on the weekend. 'This is your captain speaking! You've won a cruise! All you have to do is call us back!' You know the one that starts with a ship's foghorn blowing? Yeah, *that* one.

"I sign up for a lot of newsletters online, and I'm a sucker for filling out questionnaires for five-dollars-off coupons at the grocery store. Of course, you have to write your number down, and they sell it to third-party hacks looking to scam some jagoff. They always call twice, too. Watch, they'll call back in a few minutes." And they did.

Noble continued to read, and just as Kirk got on his moped to get revenge on his neighbor, the phone rang again. "You don't have voicemail?" he snapped.

"Nope," I said. "If someone wants to get a hold of me, they keep calling back. I used to have one, but after almost a whole year of never seeing the red light blinking on the machine, I got rid of it. Answer it if you want. It's actually a really funny auto-message."

Noble seemed to consider it briefly, but continued reading instead.

At 3:34 P.M., Noble finished the story. I felt hot with anticipation of what would come next, my skin searing and buzzing. Sweat coated my armpits and settled between my legs. All the delay tactics had been exhausted, and eternal "night night" was next. I felt as if it was exam day and I didn't have any more time to study. My future rode on whether I passed or failed.

He closed the book, walked over to where his shoes were, and put the book there. Fingerprints, I thought. It'd be easier to burn the book than clean them off. There'd be sweat on the pages from his thumbs, too. Smart man.

He came back and said he needed to go to the garage to get a knife, which was where he'd hidden them. He said it matter-of-factly, with as much remorse as a snake felt for the mouse in its stomach. I thought, *So, that's how it's going to happen. Stabbed or slit. Bleed out. The lights dim until they go out, pain all the way home, baby. Fade to black, like the* Sopranos *finale.*

What a bullshit way to finish something.

I grabbed the letter opener from between my legs and slid it up my left shirtsleeve. Cutting myself free at this point was useless. The only chance I had was to drive the blade through his chin or into his Adam's apple. Then I could fall on top of him and stab and stab and stab until he lay draining on my kitchen floor. Of course, I didn't want to do any of that. I didn't want to kill the man responsible for so much entertainment. I felt as if I were going to kill my best friend. Weird, I know, but that's how Noble felt to me: like someone I'd known for a long time and cared for very much. He was a man whose company I'd found myself enjoying despite everything he'd done to me. The last thing I wanted to do was murder the man who created my nightmares. Another insane notion: if he died, so too would any stories he had yet to create. The fear of living in a Noble-less world discouraged my need to defend myself.

Noble came back into the kitchen, holding my big kitchen knife—the one I used for cutting vegetables and prepping dinner. It was long and thin, so I figured he was just going to slit me and not stab me. It seemed like the more humane of the two.

My breath quickened. I could feel beads of sweat collecting on my forehead and running down the back of my neck. My eyes started to water—more from the stress than from sadness. I figured this was the reaction most people had when the doctor told them the results were in; it was cancer, and they had "X" amount of time to live, so sorry. I think everyone cries at that point, but they're tears of denial and anger rather than sorrow. Those tears come later.

I wiped my eyes with my good wrist. Noble's back was to me as he rinsed the knife under the tap, staring at the manuscript and running his finger down the length of the blade.

I started quivering, my mouth dry and my throat ballooning with anxiety. I'd always been afraid of death and what came after. *Especially* what came after. Either I was a bad boy and went to hell, a good boy and went to heaven, or it was blackness and I ceased to exist. What had Eric Idle said in *Life of Brian*? "You come from nothing; you're going back to nothing. What have you lost? Nothing!" True, but when you were tied to the cross, it was harder to accept.

Noble turned around and wiped the knife dry with the dish towel. He threw the cloth on the floor and put the knife on the counter, next to *my* manuscript.

"Do you have any music?" he asked. "I'd like to drown out the noise with some tunes. Anything you want to hear?"

I told him there were CDs on the shelf behind me and that I'd like to listen to "A Day in the Life" from *Sgt. Pepper's*—my "last song."

He leaned over me and reached for the pile of scattered CDs. I tightened my grip on the letter opener and tried to pull it out of my sleeve, but Noble's stomach was pressing down on my shoulder, so I couldn't raise my arm or move my elbow to free the knife. He carried a stack of CDs over to the stereo and checked each one out, then opened the case for *Sgt. Pepper's* and put it in the CD player. The first track opened with gallery chatter and the plucking of instruments being tuned. I relaxed and waited for the hammering of drums and jolt of distorted electric guitar. Noble skipped forward before the song could officially start. *Jagoff.* He skipped ahead to my favorite song, but now I really wanted to hear the whole album.

As the acoustic guitar lifted off, Noble began poking the air with his fingers, doing his best impression of playing the piano. Then he grabbed the knife and held it up, studying it, his hips swaying gently and gracefully. He was clearly a man who liked to dance. When the piano started toward the crescendo, before Lennon told you that he'd read the news today, oh boy, Noble started toward me.

He stood in front of me, holding the knife vertically, sharp edge facing me. His chest heaved in and out. A drop of sweat dribbled down his cheek. I clutched the letter opener with my right hand, waiting for him to move in close enough for me to make my move. He grabbed the hair on the top of my head and clutched it. My neck yelped, but fear trumped pain now. I was shaking, aware that one of us was going to die. He brought the knife to my throat. I moved to pull my dull blade out.

A floorboard squealed behind Noble.

We both froze, the knife pressed against the side of my neck, the smell of dish soap and sour sweat hanging in the air. The blade nicked my throat when I looked up. A man I hadn't seen in over fifteen years stood behind and off to the side of Noble—my father.

11

He held a pump-action shotgun with a tan stock and forestock pressed against Noble's right temple. He'd grown a scraggily beard. His hair hadn't thinned, but it had faded from the dark brown I'd known growing up and was now a shiny silver. For a moment, I didn't know whom to be more afraid of, my dad or Noble.

"Dad . . . Wh—wh—"

Woke up,
fell out of bed,
dragged a comb across my head.

"Just shut your mouth, Ritchie. Mister? You let that knife on that there table, an' you do it slowly. You so much as fart, an' I'll be cleanin' your skull off the other side of the kitchen n'at. Do any more than that, an' it's strike two, buster. That's all you get. Y'understand?"

Noble looked puzzle for a moment, clearly confused by the change in hardball rules, then nodded and pulled the knife away from my neck, a small drop of blood running off the blade. He put it on the table and put his hands out, palms down.

"Take exactly five steps back, away from my son," my dad ordered. "Take four or six an' your chest will look like stars in the sky. Two strikes."

Noble backed up, his head down, no doubt counting the exact steps demanded of him. When he stopped, he tried to turn his head to look at *my* manuscript.

"Up here, sonny," my dad said. "That's real good. The counter ain't your friend. Eyes over here. C'mon."

Noble stared at *my* manuscript for a few seconds longer, then reluctantly turned away from it and met my dad's eyes.

I sat as confused as the day I was born, mouth ajar in disbelief as my father stood pointing his shotgun at Evan Noble. I was flush from exhaustion. All adrenaline had ceased, and I felt as if I were suffocating.

"Ritchie," my dad said, "care to explain why this beady-eyed old neb-nose has you tied up in a chair, an' why he had a kitchen knife to your throat?"

My mouth moved to talk, but nothing came out.

Now they know
how many holes
it takes to fill
the Albert Hall.

Noble began, "Sir, I can ex—"

"You will stand there like an invalid 'less you want an ass where your face is," my dad interrupted. "One more word, jagoff. One more, an' you are fuckin' out. You'll taste gunpowder an' metal. Now turn that fuckin' noise off."

Noble hesitated, then inched backward to the CD player and fumbled the buttons until he hit stop.

"Ritchie?" my dad said. "What are yunz doin'? Time's a-wastin'."

I watched Noble with bittersweet amusement and felt embarrassed for him—a grown man reduced to a scared little boy.

"Dad, this is Evan Noble."

"The man who writes shitty stories about ghouls?"

"Yeah . . . Mr. Noble, uh . . . he thought I stole something that belonged to him. He roughed me up by mistake . . . panicked, y'know? He thought he was going to kill me, but I don't think he would have. 'Cause I was gonna take this and shove it in his throat if he meant to finish me off." I showed my dad the letter opener.

Noble stole a glance at the opener, blinked, and then returned to my dad.

I continued. "But it wouldn't have come to that. Right, Evan?" I noticed that the front of his pants was soaked and that a small yellow puddle had collected at the heel of his foot.

He nodded.

"Bullshit," my dad said.

I insisted, "This is all just a huge mistake—a series of mistakes."

"Well, I don't believe you, but that don't matter. Ritchie, you tell me what you wanna do. I'll shoot him where he stands, if you will it. Or I'll call the cops an' let *them* handle it."

Noble sniffled. I could see he was

fighting back tears. He fixed his glasses, then started sobbing, probably realizing that one way or the other, he was fucked.

My dad made a face of disgust and snickered, the butt of the gun in his shoulder, never taking his aim off of Noble.

"I don't want you to do either of those things, Dad," I said. "We're going to let him go home. We're going to let him walk out of here in his piss-stained pants, and he's going to go back to his wife and dog and forget I ever existed. Isn't that right?"

Noble blinked, his eyebrows furrowed in puzzlement. It took him a few seconds to realize what I'd said. When it clicked, Noble nodded insistently, his chin hitting his chest with each downward thrust, forcing his glasses down the bridge of his nose. He used a shaking finger to slide them back up.

My dad frowned. "If you say so, Ritchie. But mister, there's somethin' we need to attend to 'fore we send you on your way. You're gonna pay for my son's hospital bills. You're gonna send a check, a big one . . . for five hundred thousand dollars. If my son wants to keep the change, you won't say boo about it. And if that check doesn't come, the police'll find plenty of evidence to corrob'rate my son's story that you tried to kill him an' held him captive for I dunno how long. If they laugh it off, you be rest assured that I'll find you an' finish the job." He looked at me. "Richie, you got sandwich baggies?"

I nodded.

"Good," he said. "Lots o' evidence to bag up an' hold."

Noble swallowed hard.

My dad grinned.

"Secondly," my dad went on, "you'd be wise to listen to what my son said. Whenever you leave this house, you forget that he ever existed. This was all just a bad dream—one you'll keep to yourself. Y'understand?"

Noble nodded, wiping the tears from his cheeks.

"Now get outta here," my dad said, "an' don't let the door hit your ass on the way out." He grinned at his own joke.

"First," I interjected, "I'd like you to take a marker and sign every copy of your books that I own—the manuscript included. Cover page. Make them out to your good buddy, Ritchie."

Noble looked wildly around the kitchen.

"There's a beer stein with pens and markers in the living room," I said. "Leave the manuscript where you found it, by my sitting chair. Thanks. That brings us to the second item. If I end up with a blank check for a lot of money, or an envelope full of cash to pay for my medical bills, questions will be asked. The IRS might start sniffing around, and if I don't have an answer, I'll be forced to give them the only one I have. When you write out your check, think of it as a bill of sale."

Noble scrunched his face into a comically confused expression.

I added, "For the manuscript that you've 'bought' from me and are leaving here. Get it?"

Noble nodded and dragged his feet from the kitchen to the living room. My dad followed behind him, the stock of the shotgun shoved into his shoulder, the barrel pointed slightly downward to Noble's heels. I heard book after book open with a shuffle and shut with a soft *whack*. Then I heard the floor creak as Noble moved from the bookshelf to my sitting chair. Felt squeaked and scratched across the cover of *my* manuscript, followed by the thin click of the lid being returned to the marker.

He came back into the kitchen, sweating and completely defeated.

"Thanks," I said.

He nodded weakly.

"Oh, one more thing," I said. "Someone else brought it up to me, and I never thought about it until now. You chose the dumbest name for your publishing imprint on that manuscript, you know that? 'A Reasonably Important Book . . . Book'? You're like Madeline Kahn in *Young Frankenstein*: 'Tell me, exactly what is it that you *do* do?' I just thought you should know."

Noble frowned, then hung his head.

I smiled.

"Now get out," my dad growled.

Noble flinched and hopped to the front door like a gazelle. He slid his feet into his shoes, bent over to tie them, then quickly straightened up, realizing that tying them up wasn't high on the list of things to get done this minute. He reached out for the baseball bat resting against the wall beside the door.

"Just you never mind, jagoff! Y'touch that evidence an' it's strike two!" my dad barked.

Noble's hand jerked back. He snatched up his jacket, looked back toward me, then put his head down and ran outside like a dog with its tail between its legs. The screen door swung closed automatically, clipping Noble on the heel and sending him hurtling toward the stairs. He tried to grip the railing to catch his fall, but ended up doing the Superman over the flight of stairs, arms sprawled in flight before landing on his stomach and skidding across the grass. I thought he was down and out, but the resilient fucker scooped himself up and scurried to his truck.

My dad barked and slapped his knee. He walked to the front door, looked through the screen, and waved before closing the front door and locking it. Then he came into the kitchen and rested the shotgun against the fridge. Kneeling in front of me, he put his hands on my good knee.

"Ritchie, how in the hell did you end up with that jagoff? What happened, son?"

I told my dad the entire tale, from finding the manuscript to being held captive by Evan Noble.

"Jesus Christ," was all he could say.

He got up and kissed me on the forehead, brushing my sweat-thickened hair. He rested his palm on the back of my head and made me look at him. "I'm so sorry, son," he said.

Sorry for what? was all I could think. *Sorry for finally showing up when it mattered?* But who was I kidding? Better late than never.

I cut my dad off when I got to university. I was a nineteen-year-old with too many hang-ups, and he was weighing me down. One morning, I decided to end the bullshit. I called him up and told him, "You can drown if you want, but you aren't pulling me under with you."

Ten years later, my dad suffered a stroke. Not a big one, but major enough to make him take a hard look at who he was and decided to get help. Many people have these life changing things happen and never change—the cheater gets caught by his wife, realizes how much he loves her, and promises he'll never do it again, until he goes back to thinking with his dick.

When the doctors called me and told me he'd had a stroke, I didn't go to see him. He could fuck himself and rot in the deepest pits of the earth's core, for all I cared. Then, a few weeks after he was released, he called me out of the blue. I hung up on him.

He called again a week later, and this time I asked what he wanted. He said he didn't want anything. He just wanted to hear my voice. I put the receiver down and cried until my eyes burned. It had taken my dad almost thirty years to say something sweet to me.

Five years later, we still talk every Sunday at 3:00 P.M. I never missed a phone call.

I asked him now, "How did you know to come here?"

"I called at three on the button, like I always do. You didn't pick up, an' you didn't let me know that you'd be out or busy, so I thought it kinda peculiar."

Strike one.

"So, I waited five minutes. I thought maybe you was takin' a shit or a shower n'at. When you didn't pick up the second time, I started to worry."

Strike two.

"I hopped in the truck an' drove by your place. I figured I'd come up your driveway an' see if your car was here. I didn't think it would be. But when I saw it was, I knew something was wrong. When I pulled up to the side o' the house, I saw another truck—one o' them gas-guzzlers from the city.

"Don't take offense to this, son, but I know you don't have a lady friend or usually anyone comin' by other than that jagoff Perry, so I thought it was real strange. I started for the front door, but a whisper nagged at me in my head, so I went back an' got the shotgun outta my truck.

"I started to peek through your windows to see if I could spot you. Maybe you were nappin' on the couch. That's when I the blood on the floor and a man come in from the garage holdin' a huge knife.

"Fortunately, the music was on pretty loud. So, I tried the front door, but it was locked. The side door wasn't. Does it even *have* a lock?" he asked.

I shook my head. It doesn't, and for no particular reason. I just never got around to installing one. You take certain liberties when you live in the sticks surrounded by farmers and Mennonites.

"Well, count your blessin's for that," he said. "I tiptoed in, an' I tell you, Ritchie, my heart sunk to my feet when I saw how you looked. I nearly froze . . ." He paused, clearing his throat and wiping his eyes. "I snapped outta it an' stuck the cold steel o' the barrel to that man's skull. It took everythin' in me not to just pump 'n' shoot. Ritchie, why didn't you want me to hurt him?" he asked, flustered, as if I had given a complete stranger a trillion dollars.

I didn't need to think about it. "I love his books. If he's gone, there are no more coming down the pipe n'at."

Of course, my dad knew what I meant.

12

I got Evan Noble's check a week after I left the hospital.

No return address. No note with a half-assed excuse for his behavior or even an admission of guilt. Just a check made out to "Richard Favreau" in the amount of six hundred thousand dollars—a sum above what Pops had demanded (probably a figure Noble thought would keep the customer satisfied).

On the Notes line were two very satisfying and hastily scrawled words: "manuscript sale".

That was the last time I saw Evan Noble's name on anything other than his latest book. I just finished *Recover*, and I loved it!

J. DONNAIT

I picked it up at a garage sale for two bucks. Talk about a steal.

Acknowledgements

Big thanks for all of the support from my family and friends, who have both poked fun at my career choice AND purchased every new release.

Thanks, Dad, for letting us hole up in your house while I get this writing thing underway. The garden has never looked better, eh?

About the Author

J. Donnait is a Toronto-born boy who loves to play hockey, video games, and watch the same chunk of movies over and over again so that he can quote them endlessly (and accurately) to his annoyed group of friends. He also lives to make scary and weird things up for you, cool reader, to enjoy. According to him, "Thank my mom and her supply of toys for any imagination I possess."

For more information about J. Donnait, including where to find him on social media and new books he has coming out, visit the Epic Publishing website.

Since you enjoyed *Finders Bleeders*,
you may also enjoy:

In Case of
Carnage

By Gerry Griffiths
Author of the *Cryptid Zoo* series

1
CASE NUMBER:
18-01-236

Clare Carver placed her bulky forensic
kit by the body, avoiding the pool of blood
inches away from Detective Bill Hendrix's
patent leather shoes. He observed her
methodical process, jotting down specifics

in his notepad.

The victim was a teenage girl, possible runaway. Skin smooth as Philadelphia cream cheese. Black Hot Topic T-shirt with a crudely cut hole haloing a green barbell belly button ring. Designer blue jeans fashionably snipped away at the knees. Red Keds high-tops without shoelaces. Green spiked hair in the rust-colored blood on the cement floor.

Bill crouched to inspect the weepy quarter-inch hole in her forehead, the gold shield on his belt digging into his gut. He noticed puncture marks on the girl's neck, just under her right ear.

"Are those incisor wounds on her throat?"

Clare leaned forward for a closer look. "Possibly."

"Too clean for an animal bite."

"What are you suggesting?"

"I'd say it's the work of a vampire."

Clare gave him an incredulous look before bursting into laughter.

"Better not let Hank hear you say that." Clare glanced at Bill's gun. "Is that a snub-nosed thirty-eight?"

"Smith and Wesson. Same as Hank

carries. Why?"

"They still make those? When are you guys going to get with the latest department issue?"

"What, those plastic guns? No thanks." Bill shook his head, noting Clare's firearm strapped to her side.

Clare pulled her handgun with slick precision. "You're looking at a Glock 29 ten-millimeter with a ten-round clip, polymer frame, and non-corrosive coating, so it won't rust like those pea-shooters you two call guns," she bragged before holstering her weapon. "Standard issue, per the captain."

"Hey, a *lot* of famous detectives carried thirty-eights. *Dragnet's* Sergeant Joe Friday, Jim Rockford in *The Rockford Files.*"

"Bill, those guys weren't even real cops. Please don't tell me you're packing those three-eighty automatics around your ankles."

"They're great little backup guns."

"Next you're going to tell me you use speedloaders." She laughed, patting the two ten-round clips on her belt next to the tactical folding knife in a Velcro sheath beside her holstered high-tech semi-automatic.

Bill was about to reach into his jacket pocket when a mall security guard came into the room looking like he had just left his mother's funeral.

"What are you two squabbling about?" Detective Hank Jenkins entered the storeroom right behind the despondent security guard. Hank slipped the man's firearm in an evidence bag.

"Where's Silverman?" Bill asked. Normal protocol required that the first uniformed officer on the crime scene be present to answer questions during the primary investigation.

"Other side of the mall. Checking surveillance."

"Bill thinks the girl was bitten by a vampire." Clare pointed at the dead girl's neck.

"Jeez, Bill. Can't you be serious for one minute?"

The disgruntled mall guard glanced at the dead girl, then stared down at his boots. "I can't believe it. I take this lousy job to subsidize my pissant retirement, and look what happens."

"Bill, this is Ralph Talbert," Hank said.

Bill nodded at the security guard.

Hank said to Ralph, "Tell my partner

what you told me."

Ralph cleared his throat. "The last few days there have been a number of break-ins in the mall."

Bill asked, "Why didn't the mall manager report them?"

"Maybe he was in on it. I don't know."

"Go on."

"They cut the padlocks on the metal gates, crawl under and jimmy the entry doors. So far, they've broken into about eight different stores."

Bill asked, "What are they after?"

"Well, it's weird. This mall's got tons of electronics stores, stuff you could make good money selling at the flea market. These guys? They take clothes. They've even raided the kitchens in the food court."

"How are they getting into the mall if the outside doors are locked?"

"Personally, I think it's an employee who has access to a master key." Ralph glanced over at the dead girl. "I swear, one of them was pointing a gun at me."

Hank asked, "What do you mean, 'one of them'?"

"There were two."

Hank gave Ralph a hard stare.

Ralph shrugged. "Jesus, I thought I told you."

A loud crash came from the main floor of the sporting goods store.

"What was that?" Bill snatched his gun out of the shoulder rig.

Hank stuffed Ralph's gun into the side pocket of his coat. He drew his .38 snub-nosed out of the holster clipped to his belt.

Clare threw back the slide on her Glock.

Hank and Bill went first. Clare stepped out next with Ralph trailing behind her.

The sporting goods showroom was cast in shadows. A majority of the over-head fluorescent panels were turned off to conserve energy.

Hank spotted movement to his right. He signaled Bill and Clare.

A scrawny teenager stood in front of a smashed display case, shoving small boxes into a rucksack.

"Let's see those hands!" Bill barked. "This is the—"

The kid swiveled around with a shot-gun. The muzzle flash lit up as the boom thundered in the room. Bill shoved Clare to the floor and dove on top of her. Pumping another cartridge into the chamber, the gunman swung the barrel and blasted again. A rack of sleeping bags exploded in a goose down blizzard.

Hank fired a quick shot, striking the kid in the shoulder. The impact sent him toppling into the display case.

Bill got up. Clare sprang to her feet.

"I only winged him," Hank cautioned.

The teenage boy lay on the floor amid ammunition boxes covered with glass shards. Hank kicked the shotgun out of the kid's reach. Bill and Clare kept their guns trained on the suspect.

"Please don't kill me," the kid begged.

"You're lucky we didn't." Bill grabbed the shotgun off the floor.

"Wait a minute. You're not them."

"Who did you *think* we were?"

"Aw man, you're the cops!"

"Hey, where's Ralph?" Hank turned, scouting the store for the security guard.

"Over there." Clare pointed.

Ralph was dead on the floor, sprawled under the glow of a ceiling light. His face was a bloody pulp, riddled with buckshot, looking like the inside of a pomegranate.

Hank stared at the wounded teenager. "You screwed up big time, son."

Bill bent down to scrutinize the boy. "He's got the same bite marks on his neck as the girl."

A red blossom bloomed on the boy's shirt. The bullet had struck the right deltoid a couple of inches away from the shoulder.

Clare holstered her Glock. "I need to stop the bleeding." She took a pair of blue gloves out of her pants pocket. She stretched the elastic before slipping them on. "Hand me one of those shirts for a compress."

Bill grabbed a shirt off a rack. Clare wadded it up and placed it over the wound. She took the boy's left hand and pressed it palm-side down on the compress. "What's your name?"

"Peter."

"Okay, Peter. Keep applying pressure."

Clare glanced down at the boy's right arm. "Guys, look at this."

Two puncture marks on the forearm, too large for needle tracks.

"Jesus, Peter," Clare said, "Who did this to you?"

"The vampires."

Hank shook his head. "Kid, you're in enough trouble. What are you even doing in here?"

"We thought it would be cool to hide out in the mall after it closed."

"When was that?"

"I don't know. A week ago?"

Hank saw the surprised looks on Bill and Clare's faces. "Weren't you afraid of getting caught?"

"We'd smoked a bunch of weed."

"So who's your girlfriend?"

"Sissy."

"Tell us about the bite marks."

Peter must have pressed too hard on his wound because he crinkled up his face. "They feed on us. I'm a donor. Sissy's a blood doll. They take turns, pass us around like a bottle of Jim Beam."

"So you and Sissy broke into those stores?"

"Yes, they made us."

Hank frowned. "What do you mean, 'made you'? Sounds to me like you could have escaped any time you wanted."

"They have my sister. They're holding her hostage. If we don't do what they want, they'll kill her."

"What's your sister's name?"

"Peg. We needed the gun to rescue her."

"How many of these . . ." Hank paused,

rolling his eyes at Bill, "*Vampires* would you say there are?"

"Four. I'm telling you, they're crazy." Peter's eyes widened. "These guys are stronger than shit!" He raised his head off the floor to gaze around. "Hey, where's Sissy?"

Bill broke the news. "Your girlfriend is dead. The guard you killed shot her."

Peter scrunched his eyes shut, tears leaking down his cheeks.

Hank asked, "Where are they keeping your sister?"

"Under the mall."

"How do we find her?"

"Follow the corridor at the food court to the restrooms. The 'Employees Only' door to the right of the men's room is unlocked. Take the stairs down to the basement. There's a huge tunnel the delivery trucks use. Go right until you see a big 'W2' stenciled on the wall to your left with a black door. Their hideout is in there."

Bill scowled. "You know, we have a problem."

Hank let out a sigh. "And what is that?"

"They're vampires."

"This is a bunch of bull."

"You know bullets won't kill them."

"My Glock will," Clare chimed in.

"That might slow them down a bit"—Bill raised his eyebrows—"until the lead pops out of their bodies. There're only four ways you can kill a vampire." He counted them off on his fingers. "Drive a stake through their heart, cut off their head, expose them to sunlight, or set them on fire."

"I can't believe I'm standing here listening to this nonsense," Hank said. "Let's go find these jokers."

Clare used her cell phone to call the security office. She told Officer Silverman to get back to the sporting goods store, on the double to watch Peter. She then called dispatch to summon an ambulance and notify the captain of their situation. Hank handcuffed Peter's right hand to a pole next to the display case.

"Don't move. Someone will be here shortly." Clare stripped off her gloves.

They hustled out of the sporting goods store and dashed down the wide corridor that separated the specialty shops. Officer Silverman was already jogging in their direction and gave them a wave.

After reaching the food court, they

headed for the restrooms. Hank spotted the door: Employees Only. It was unlocked, so he pushed it open. Cement stairs stretched down into the tenebrous gloom of the underground tunnels. He started down, Bill a step behind, Clare taking up the rear.

Halfway down, Hank heard a crack. He glanced over his shoulder. "What was that?"

Bill held up what looked like a stick.

"Is that an arrow?"

"Yeah, I broke off the metal tip."

"Why?"

"The shaft has to be made solely of wood when driven through a vampire's heart."

Hank looked at what Bill had in his other hand. "You took a crossbow?"

"Yeah, I grabbed it on our way out of the store, along with some arrows." Bill pulled another arrow out of the short quiver that was sticking out of the side pocket of his jacket. He pressed the end against the concrete wall, snapping the tip off.

"Jesus, I don't believe you!" Hank continued down.

Clare tapped Bill on the shoulder. "Jeez, Bill. You're really serious about this."

"Clare, they're vampires."

"You know, it might not hurt to have a little chat with the departmental shrink."

"Why? 'Cause you're dating him?"

"No, I'm not!"

"Not what *I* heard."

"Okay, we went out *once*, but—"

Hank barked from the bottom of the stairs, "Will you two keep it down!"

Clare and Bill rushed down the steps and joined Hank. They stood in the middle of a large tunnel with loading docks stretching in both directions, tapering into the darkness.

"The only way to gain access from the outside is through one of those entrances, which are controlled by the guard in the security office." Hank pointed to an automatic roll-up door.

The tunnel was nearly twenty feet high—wide enough for two big rig trailers to squeeze past each other going in opposite directions. A network of yellow globe lights, various-sized plumbing pipes, and conduits of electrical wiring ran along the ceiling. The nearest loading dock had the store's name stenciled on the side of the concrete ramp.

Farther on they found the black door next to the large "W2" painted on the wall.

Hank stood on one side of the door, one hand on the handle. Bill and Clare steeled themselves against the wall.

Hank flung open the door. They stormed in—Hank sweeping left, Clare taking the right, and Bill up the middle—panning their guns about the large room. It looked like a den for the homeless. Filthy sleeping bags were strewn across the floor. Black garbage bags bulged with stolen merchandise. Empty food containers were tossed in a corner. Trash was scattered everywhere. The stale, putrid air reeked of body odor and filthy clothes.

The room was deserted.

"Maybe they heard the gunshots." Bill kicked a shoebox across the floor.

"I heard something!" Clare bolted out of the room. The two detectives charged out after her.

"There they are!" Clare pointed to two figures racing down the tunnel.

A scream came from the opposite direction.

"Damn, they split up," Hank said. "Bill, Clare, go that way. I'll follow these two."

* * *

They were faster than a pair of doped-up track runners. The way they ran reminded Hank of apes loping in the jungle. The sounds of their feet slapping the pavement let him know they were barefoot. Probably didn't have time to put on shoes. He wondered if they were armed.

His legs were already starting to burn. He needed to get back to his routine morning jogs, devote fewer hours behind the desk.

Hank slowed as he reached a bend in the tunnel. If they were smart, they would wait in ambush, attack when he came running blindly around the corner.

He stopped for a second to listen. He could hear air flowing through the ducts above his head, liquid surging down the pipes. Somewhere behind the walls, machines hummed, busy at work.

Hank slid along the concrete wall, edging around the bend. He found himself standing below the loading dock with the sporting goods store logo.

A forklift was parked on one side of the huge platform. Empty pallets were stacked high against a wall near a control panel for a giant gray compactor—the kind for flattening cardboard boxes. The twin doors remained open on the hopper, like crushing jaws waiting for a victim.

Half a dozen pallets stood in front of the closed door of the receiving area with merchandise covered in shrink-wrap. Hank pointed his .38, climbing the short flight of concrete steps leading to the platform. He crept past the forklift to the first pallet.

He could see the labels through the shrink-wrap: boxed camping stoves and cases of kerosene. He squeezed between two more pallets stacked high with boxes. It was like being wedged inside a narrow passage. A pallet skidded toward Hank, threatening to crush him against the pallet directly behind him.

...

If you'd like to read on, visit our website for links to *In Case of Carnage* at your favorite online retailers or visit your local bookstore to ask them to order a copy for you.

Notes from the Publisher

We hoped you enjoyed reading this book as much as we did. Please help the author by leaving a review on your favorite online retailer, Goodreads, or BookBub.

Mighty Quill Books

Follow the Mighty Quill Books blog to get book news and inside information about our authors.